CaiRo JiM
ON THE TRaiL To
CHaCHa MUCHOS

CAIRO JIM
ON THE TRAIL TO
CHACHA MUCHOS

An Epic Tale of Rhythm

GEOFFREY MCSKIMMING

Hodder
Children's
Books
Australia

A Hodder Children's Book

This edition published in Australia and New Zealand in 1994
by Hodder Headline Australia Pty Limited,
(A member of the Hodder Headline Group)
Level 22, 201 Kent Street, Sydney NSW 2000
Website: www.hha.com.au

First published in 1992
Reprinted 1992, 1993
Reprinted in this edition 1996, 1997, 1999, 2001 (twice)

Copyright © Text Geoffrey McSkimming 1992

National Library of Australia Cataloguing-in-Publication data

McSkimming, Geoffrey, 1962- .
Cairo Jim on trail to ChaCha Muchos

ISBN 0 340 56683 3.

I. Title.

A823.3

Typeset by G.T. Setters Pty Ltd, Kenthurst, NSW
Printed in Australia by Griffin Press

GEOFFREY McSKIMMING

When Geoffrey McSkimming was a boy he found an old motion-picture projector and a tin containing a dusty film in his Grandmother's attic. He screened the film and was transfixed by the flickering image of a man in a jaunty pith helmet, baggy Sahara shorts and special desert sun-spectacles. The man had an imposing macaw and a clever-looking camel, and Geoffrey McSkimming was mesmerised by their activities in black-and-white Egypt, Peru, Greece, and other exotic locations.

Years later he discovered the identities of the trio, and he has spent much of his time since then retracing their footsteps, interviewing surviving members of the Old Relics Society, and gradually reconstructing these lost true tales which have become the enormously successful Cairo Jim Chronicles.

Cairo Jim on the Trail to ChaCha Muchos was written after Geoffrey McSkimming spent a month in Peru, where he trekked the rugged Inca Trail, camped in the Amazonian rainforest jungles, and partook of several goluptious Kahuzis in the legendary Popocatepetl Club.

Thankfully, he did not meet Captain Neptune Bone.

It's yet another
Cairo Jim
Mystery of History

CONTENTS

For Belinda, with all my love

PRELUDE

IN the midnight-tangled jungle of a mountain far
from time, in the dark, leafy shadows, a bedraggled
tribe of Indians huddle around a small fire, their eyes
and ears wearily alert as once again, for one more night,
they wait patiently.

The flames crackle into the quiet night; they leap
up and throw long, slanted beams on the faces of those
nearest the warmth. High above, an enormous canopy
of leaves, vines and darkened flowers blot the stars from
view.

Occasionally a squirrel monkey shrieks out from
the darkness, his rapid chatter ratter-tatting like gunfire
into the flickering gloom of the clearing. Then there
is a colossal flutter of thousands of pairs of wings,
followed by uncountable noises of birdstartle, and then
just as suddenly the jungle returns to silence.

All around the fire, tired eyes stare from tired faces.
Some of the smaller white-haired children have fallen
asleep and are nestled into their mothers' backs, snug
in their colourful sleeping bundles. These children have
wizened little faces and rough little hands and, if you
were to walk into this clearing right now and look

at them, you would probably think they were very old human beings. And if you were then to look at the older members of the tribe with their unwrinkled faces and their soft fingers, you would probably think they were very young human beings. Tired, but young. For it is a curious characteristic of this tribe that the older they become, the younger they appear.

The boy Yupichu is beginning to look younger. In recent months his fingers have lost many of their notches and the skin on his face has become smoother. His hair, too, is slowly changing colour, becoming less white and more grey. The process which will last for the rest of his life has begun. Yupichu has come of age. It is time for him to ask questions.

He has been waiting for this night for a long time. There are many questions he wants to ask Zapateado, who is sitting next to him, staring into the fire. Yupichu has been storing the questions in his mind for many seasons. Whenever he could not sleep he would dwell on them for hours and hours, imagining the night when it would be his turn, his *right*, to begin asking them. Sometimes his curiosity had been so intense it was as though somebody was holding a glowing ember from the fire behind his forehead. There were so many questions he wanted, *needed* to ask.

But one particular question had remained on the top shelf of his mind. It had kept bobbing up, kept flooding into him, usually at those moments before the Keeper of Slumbers would come. Then Yupichu would open his eyes and stare up at the breeze-whispering canopy and remain wide awake with frustration coursing through him because he did not know the answer. Over the years this question had become a great taunt to the boy. It had teased him and taunted him; it had made him angry and impatient. Above all it had planted in him the seeds of determination to ask Zapateado.

Zapateado was the one to ask. He was the Teller of All That Had Been. He was the Keeper of the Past. He had the blackest hair of all the tribe.

The boy took a deep breath and sucked the cool air of the forest, with its scents of rain and leaves and pollens, deeply into his lungs. He reached out and touched the shoulder of the old man. 'Zapateado! Zapateado!'

The old man continued to stare into the flames. He did not seem to hear Yupichu. He did not move at all.

'Zapateado! It is me, Yupichu.'

There was the tiniest flicker across Zapateado's face, as though a humming bird had beaten its wings very close and had caused a small breeze of air to fan towards him.

'I hear you, boy,' he said, his lips barely moving.

'I have come of age. See, I am changing. Look at me.'

Zapateado did not look away from the fire. 'I have seen,' he said. 'I have observed these things in you in recent months.'

Yupichu crouched on his haunches and held his hands tightly around his knees until his knuckles began to turn white. 'One day,' he whispered, 'I will look like you.'

'That day is a long time to come. Many rains will

fall before then. Speak to me, boy. Do not waste breath. It is precious.'

'You are the Keeper of the Past.'

Zapateado felt for the small leather pouch hanging from his woven belt. 'That I am,' he said.

'You are the Teller of All That Has Been.'

'That I am.'

Yupichu took a huge breath. 'Tonight I must ask you something, something I——'

Zapateado raised his hand and turned his broad, smooth palm towards the boy's face. 'I have seen in your eyes the hunger to ask this question,' he said. 'The question I know not, but your hunger to ask it I have tasted. Ask me, Yupichu. Ask me and I shall give you the answer, if it is within my Knowing.'

The boy leaned back and rested on the balls of his heels. His forehead glistened with beads of moisture. He took another deep breath. 'Why, every year when the rains come, do we go up *there*?'

The smooth-skinned, dark-haired man began to tingle in every pore of his skin, for it was again time to tell another youthing boy the story which in itself told the history of their tribe. The story of why they were here this evening. Why they were waiting. The story of why they had waited so many evenings during so many years...

Zapateado turned to the boy, his eyes carrying the flames of the fire. It was time to tell Yupichu of the One who, guided by the mystery of the mountainous nights and the lure of the music in her head, had stepped out of this human world one night almost half a millennium ago into an Eternity all her own. The

One they now called their Awaited: the All-Seeing,
All-Knowing, All-Dancing Sandra the Celestial.
    Sandra of the Heavens.
    She Who Will Return...

1

FLYING WITH THE VALKYRIES

THE propellers of the great silver aeroplane were droning like a thousand earnest wasps through the wispy cotton-wool clouds when all at once Cairo Jim was woken from his slumber by a voice that was cool and confident and warmly familiar to him.

'It's about time we crossed paths again,' this voice said.

The archaeologist–poet shifted his pith helmet and looked up. There in the aisle, wearing her Valkyrian Airways Flight Attendant uniform, stood his friend Jocelyn Osgood. He stood to shake her hand. 'Hello, there,' he smiled. 'I was hoping you might be on this flight.'

'It's wonderful to see you again, Jim,' she smiled back. 'I was beginning to think you'd stopped flying Valkyrian.'

'Oh, no, never. It's the only way to travel.'

'Of course it is. And how are the poems going?'

'I'm still writing them. Although I haven't had any published yet.'

'Still, it's good to be able to discover things, isn't it? I do envy you that. My, that's a jaunty pith helmet. New, is it?'

'Actually——'

'I didn't think I'd seen it before. Now sit down and tell me why you're going to Peru. Would you like some tea?'

'As a matter of fact——'

'I won't be a flash.' And away she hovered up the aisle.

It had been a little while since he had last seen her, and her face, which hadn't changed at all really, was like something new and fresh to him.

(There were some small orchestras, especially those from parts of the Tyrol, who thought that Jocelyn Osgood had a very striking face. She herself, however, thought she had a very *practical* face: her eyes were set at just the right distance from each other so that flying goggles—which she wore whenever parachuting or piloting small aeroplanes—sat at just the right angle; her ears did not protrude too much from beneath her horned Valkyrian beret; her nose fitted snugly into the oxygen masks she had to demonstrate at the beginning of every flight; and her mouth covered her numerous pearly teeth. All of this arrangement was framed by her unusually vibrant, curly auburn hair which often gave her bother, usually after she had washed it. She mostly wore this pulled back in a tight bun and tried not to think about it too much.)

Soon she returned with a large silver teapot and two cups and saucers. She poured the tea, handed one across to Jim at the window, and sat on the armrest of the empty seat next to him. 'So,' she said. 'Why Peru?'

Jim stirred his tea. 'Lima's the starting point,' he replied. 'From there it's out to Cuzco.'

'And from there?'

'Who knows?'

Jocelyn's eyes lit up. 'Another expedition?' she asked eagerly.

Jim nodded.

'And what are you after this time?' she whispered.

He looked carefully around to ensure there were no eavesdroppers. When he was sure it was all right he leaned towards her. 'A city,' he whispered back.

'Really?' Her eyes locked on his special desert sun-spectacles. Tell me more, they seemed to be saying. . .

He rested his cup and saucer on the armrest near the window and reached down underneath his seat. 'A city which, if it exists, may be of the most extraordinary archaeological importance,' he said, delving into his leather knapsack.

'*If* it exists?'

'If it exists,' he repeated. He sat upright once again and placed a large, old, green leather-bound book upon his lap. 'Let me show you,' he said, his voice trembling slightly with excitement. With moist fingers he opened the thick volume to a page marked by a long, scrawny, black-as-pitch feather.

'Strange bookmark,' Jocelyn observed.

'Mmm. It was in the book when Gerald Perry Esquire showed it to me in the Old Relics Society library. Ah, here we are. Feast your eyes, Miss Osgood.'

He spread the book fully flat on his knees. Jocelyn leaned closer and looked carefully at the black-and-white engraving.

There in front of her, rising up and away into a sky laced with misty clouds, was a range of mountains, all of them volcanic in appearance, all of them covered with thick, dense jungle. On the peak of the tallest and craggiest of these mountains, carved out of the rock face, perched an ancient city. The roughly hewn buildings stretched far out across the mountain ridges, and the stone towers and buttresses built high on the rocky outcrops reminded Jocelyn in some way of the spikes on the back of a long extinct dinosaur.

'That's what I'm going to find,' Jim said confidently.

Jocelyn looked at the bottom of the page. There she read the neat, old-fashioned lettering:

ChaCha Muchos

Lost City of the Dancers

'Well, I'll be. . .' she muttered.

'Of course, it's only an artist's impression,' said Jim quickly. 'No-one's seen it in the last five hundred years or so, so there's no telling *what* it might look like today.'

'I've never heard of it,' Jocelyn said, running her index finger slowly along her lower lip. 'Never even read of it. . .'

'Neither had I, until Gerald Perry found this book. I don't think too many others have read of it either, judging from the dust.' He slapped the page heavily, causing a small white mushroom-cloud of fine particles to blow straight up into Jocelyn's face.

Jocelyn pulled out her handkerchief and clamped the polka-dotted silk over her nose. 'Ah. . .ah. . .ah,' she sniffled.

'Let me read you some of what it says.' He turned back a few pages—being careful of the dust—until he found what he was after. 'Ah. Here we are.'

He began reading in a quiet, eager voice:

Chapter Thirty-Eight, 'ChaCha Muchos: The Lost City of the Dancers'

In the Fifteenth Century, the town of Cuzco was known the world over as a lively and cheerful place. Its streets were always filled with flowers and dancing people, and its shops were renowned for their beautifully woven shawls, their finely crafted straw hats, their unique macramè llama bridles, and the most famous thing of all: the Cuzco Clackersmacker, a nectareous round sweetie which was the delicacy of peasant and prince and princess. So popular was this confectionery that traders would often place their lives in peril to venture through dark, savage jungles to exchange gold, silver and diamonds for sacks full of the little sweet balls.

'Goodness,' said Jocelyn. 'They must have been delicious.'

'They certainly must've been,' Jim said. 'And popular. Listen to what happened:'

The people of Cuzco were happy in their town, totally free from the bother of war and the worry of invasion. They were so happy that, as time passed, they devoted less and less time to the manufacture of their beautifully woven shawls and finely crafted straw hats and unique macramè llama bridles and even the Cuzco Clackersmacker, preferring instead to spend every spare moment of their days and nights dancing around in the cobbled streets.

'Oh, dear,' muttered Jocelyn Osgood.
'It gets worse.' He continued:

It so happened that the King of Spain was a great eater of these goluptious delights. When his traders returned to court one day with news that there were no more Clackersmackers to be had in the whole of Cuzco, indeed, in the whole of Peru, because the citizens would do nothing but dance, he flew into a furious rage, tearing his crown from his royal head and hurling it at the nearest courtiero. For a month he sulked in his royal bedroom, whingeing for Clackersmackers. Then, determined not to be forevermore deprived of his succulent goodies, he sent a fleet of ships to Peru, one of which carried a Decree that would forcibly change the lifestyles of the idle and unenterprising citizens of Cuzco.

The fleet anchored some months later in Callao harbour near Lima. When they arrived in this city, the King's conquistadors heard stories about the Cuzconians that made their hairs curl beneath their morions. They set out through the jungles in haste.

After an arduous and sometimes dangerous trek lasting nearly two months, the conquistadors reached Cuzco. Without warning, and being totally unexpected by the dancing citizens, they invaded the small town and pasted the King's Decree on every corner of every plaza. The people of Cuzco were horrified.

'What did this Decree decree?'
'Let me see...ah, here it is:'

The Decree of the King of Spain decreed that all Cuzconian frivolity was to cease immediately, that all dancing would from that moment be regarded as an offence of the most criminal kind, and that henceforth the people of Cuzco were to settle down to a life of orderliness, sensibleness and productivity. It further ordered that if the manufacture of shawls, hats, macramè llama bridles and Cuzco Clackersmackers (this last item was in very large letters on each poster) did not resume immediately, the entire town would be burned to the ground by the conquistadors' torches and the citizens would find themselves homeless.

'Barbaric,' Jocelyn said, tapping her fingertips together thoughtfully.

Jim continued:

Most of the Cuzconians promptly came to their senses. They threw away their dancing shoes and returned to work. As time went on, they forgot their terpsichorean ways and managed to find new happiness and pride in their world-famous crafted merchandise. However, not *all* the people of Cuzco were so eager to give up their former practices. There was a small group in the community for whom dancing was the most important thing of all. These people could not imagine their lives without the Dance and, when they read the royal Decree, they knew there was only one thing to do. They banded together in a conspiratorial manner and, one quiet, moonlit night, they dosidoed away, escaping under the very noses of the conquistadors.

'What became of these rebels?'

Jim snapped the book shut and quickly fanned the rising dust away with his hand. 'Ah. They went up into the mountains surrounding Cuzco and built their very own city in a place that was so secluded, so remote, so impossible to find that no-one ever has.' He leaned back and shut his eyes. 'ChaCha Muchos,' he murmured dreamily. 'The Lost City of the Dancers...'

Jocelyn stared out through the aircraft windows, her eyes seeming to take in every molecule of the atmosphere outside. 'Goodness,' she breathed. 'I wonder how they did it.'

Cairo Jim opened his eyes and gave a small frown. 'It goes on to say that according to local legend, the Dancers met up with a group of Indians who gave them some kind of potion which they used to carve out the rock face. Apparently the potion could dissolve everything except leather. It's all a lot of bunkum if you ask me.'

'I wonder.' She leaned back and clasped her skirted knee and said, 'Where do you think ChaCha Muchos might be?'

He sipped his tea as he thought. 'Looking at maps, and going on the engraving, I'd say somewhere north of Cuzco. The mountains there rise up out of the jungles. The only problem is, *which* mountain...'

They were interrupted by a crackle and a sudden voice coming from the front of the aircraft: 'Attention, ladies and gentlemen and everyone else. This is your Captain, Erik Odin, speaking. In approximately a few short hours we will be landing in Lima, Peru. I would like to advise all passengers that Peruvian time is eight hours behind our present time, so would you please adjust your timepieces accordingly. Thank you, and on behalf of the crew, I hope you are having a pleasant flight with Valkyrian, the airline that always flies over the top.'

Jim busied himself with his Cutterscrog Old Timers Archaeological Timepiece while Jocelyn unstrapped her own wristwatch.

'Is that the right time?' she asked, glancing at his dial. 'Heavens, I seem to be running an hour slow.'

They simultaneously wound back their watches to Peruvian time.

'New watch, Jim?'

'Mmm,' he mmmed. 'A gift from Gerald Perry. It's a genuine Cutterscrog, you know.'

'Very nice.' She strapped her watch back onto her wrist. 'Jim?'

'Mmm?'

'I think I might be able to introduce you to someone who may be of some help in finding the City.'

'Oh, yes?'

'Yes. A woman I met recently. Dolores. That's her name. Dolores del Tempo. Everyone calls her "Miss del Tempo" though, except me. She's quite all right, will do anything for you if it's sensible. She knows quite a lot about Peruvian history.'

Jim was interested. 'Where do we find this woman?'

'She's a singer and solo violinist at one of the better clubs in Lima. We'll go and see her tomorrow night, if you'd like.'

'Yes,' Jim said. 'I'd like that very much.' He gazed out of the window. 'How about that,' he thought. 'Miss Dolores del Tempo. A contact already.'

He looked down, far down through the thinning

wisps of cloud, to the dark ocean. There, in the middle of all the watery nowhere, he spied a tiny dot belching thick black smoke into the endless nothingness of the sky.

2

DARK ENTERPRISE

IT was a smallish vessel, barnacled and steam-powered, with a belching, grimy, green funnel. Across the starboard side its name could still be read, even though the dull grey paint was flaking miserably. Normally this decrepit, creaking ship transported Egyptian prunes between Cairo and Lima—hot, steamy, shrivelled things piled squashingly into the cavernous, rat-infested hold—but on this particular voyage it was not prune laden. Instead, the entire ship had been chartered by that dubious archaeologist, Captain Neptune Bone.

Now twilight was beginning to descend in a fog the colour of honey. The bearded Captain stretched his stout legs out in front of him and blew an acrid column of cigar smoke towards a slurping black object in the opposite corner of the only passenger-cabin.

'Do you know,' he rumbled, his voice vibrating against the slatted wooden blinds over the portholes, 'that there are more golden artefacts in the Cairo Museum than in any other single place in the entire world?'

The ship lurched sharply as it rode the swell, and there was a sudden jerk from the slurping black object. An empty seaweed tin rolled away and clattered against the far wall.

'Did you hear me, bird?' snarled Bone.

An eye appeared, red and throbbing, from somewhere at the top of the blackness. Then a beak opened and Bone saw the rough, yellow tongue of his companion, the raven, Desdemona.

'Craaarrk! I hear,' she croaked.

'Arrr. And do you remember those gargantuan doors at the entrance of this most lucrative location?'

From one of her black-as-pitch feathers she pecked out a flea. She had a bit of a chew on it—it was a big, fat, juicy one this time—then spat it onto the wooden floor. 'I do, I do, I do,' she throbbed.

'I have studied those doors closely on nights when I have attended Old Relics Society cheese and cracker functions at the Museum. They are impenetrable, let me tell you.'

'Nothing is impenetrable,' the raven spat.

'Your skull is,' Bone sneered. 'That's why they couldn't get a brain into it.'

'At least I don't have a head full of custard.'

'What did you say?' His tone was threatening.

She looked up at the awesome man in his ochre-coloured fez, emerald green waistcoat, and magnolia-coloured plus-fours trousers, and her eyes throbbed harder. He was a distasteful sight, she thought.

'I asked you what did you say?'

'I said I can't help it if it's busted.'

'What?'

'My skull. I can't help it if it's —— '

'Arrrr, I'm sure that's not what you said at all.' He puffed indignantly on his tobacco. 'I'd be extremely careful if I were you,' he rumbled slowly. 'Remember, if it weren't for me, the Antiquity Squad would have had its way with you by now...'

'Craaaark! Nevermore.'

'It's still not too late. If you don't display a little courtesy you might find yourself a feather duster before too long.'

'What would I need to find a feather duster for?'

'Malevolent moron.'

'Craaaark!'

'As I was saying, those doors have, up until now, proved to be a most frustrating obstacle to such an enterprising genius such as what I am. If it weren't for those massive portals of prevention, I could have been the richest archaeologist in the world by now. But soon, bird, all that will change.'

'Oh yes?' The raven sounded sceptical.

'You bet your barbules it will.' He stroked his ginger-brown beard and smirked. 'And I will have wealth far beyond your wildest nightmares.'

'Just how,' she said haughtily, 'will you manage that?'

'Tell me once again what you read in that book in the Society's library.'

She rolled her eyeballs and sighed. This would be the eighth time since they had left Cairo that he had asked her to repeat this information. He was definitely up to something. 'What part of the story?' she asked wearily.

'The bit about that potion.' He closed his eyes and waited.

She cleared her seaweedy throat and quoted in a chanting rhythm:

The dancing escapees from Cuzco ventured through the cloudforested jungles where it is said they stumbled across an ancient Indian tribe who possessed a rare and hitherto unknown potion. This potion was capable of dissolving every substance known to humans, the only exception being leather. In return for teaching the tribe some sprightly new dance steps, the Cuzconians were given a small gourd of this potion which, it is believed, they used to carve out their city—known in local legends as 'ChaCha Muchos'—high atop a foliage-covered mountain.

Bone opened his eyes. 'Are you quite positive that's what it said?'

'Word for word. A direct quote, exactly.' She hopped up and down, trying to shake out a flea that was being troublesome in a tender spot.

'How can you be so sure?'

'Birds have very good memories for words,' she croaked. 'That's why human beings often teach us how to talk.'

Bone clenched his cigar between his teeth and pressed the tips of his manicured fingers gently together. 'So, my foul-feathered fiend, suppose that we were able to get our hands on this fantastic potion. Imagine what we could do with it...'

Desdemona's eyes lit up. 'We could zap off all my fleas.'

'No, you pot-pourri of pestilence, I was thinking on a much larger scale.'

'Ratso.'

'Imagine the doors of the Cairo Museum. A single drop of this flabbergasting formula and—hey, presto—

they are no more. Poof! Vanished into some unknown vaporous place. And inside the Museum, all that glittering, dazzling gold, waiting there in those darkened corridors, just waiting for someone with a genius streak such as what I have to come in and cart it all away and then melt it down to be sold on some out-of-town country's black market...' He licked his excited lips and purred. 'Instant, glorious wealth...oh, the very thought of it!'

'So that's your game then?'

'A game,' Bone said smugly, 'is something one plays for pleasure. No, querulous quills, what I have is a *plan*. Something I am pursuing for profit.'

Desdemona flicked out her tongue and slurped a lump of seaweed which clung to the outside of her beak. Then she craaaaaarrrked hideously.

'Aaaarrr,' moaned Neptune Bone, covering his ears with his hands. 'What's set your merriment meter off?'

Her eyes became mocking slits and her beak took on a sinister leer. 'It's all very clever when you tell it like that,' she gloated. 'All so simple. But I have a question.'

'Ask it, cantankerous claws.'

'Where are you going to start looking? There are more jungle-covered mountains in certain parts of Peru than I have fleas.'

'Ha. I doubt that.'

'I don't. There're more than you can poke a stick at.'

'I don't have time to waste poking sticks at mountains.'

'So where are you going to start looking?'

The large man wriggled in his armchair and, with some careful manoeuvring, managed to cross his legs. 'I know perfectly well there is an abundance of mountains in Peru. That is why, as soon as we berth in Lima, we are going to pay a visit to the Popocatepetl Club.'

'Why?' snapped Desdemona.

'Because there is a woman there who, so I've heard, knows quite a lot about Peruvian history. With a tad of fortune she should be able to point us in the right direction.'

'What's her name?'

Bone thought for a second. 'Del Tempo, I believe. Dolores del Tempo, or some such thing.'

'Bleccch,' the raven gurgled. 'Do we have to see her? Human beings, especially *women* human beings, really don't take to me.'

'Would you rather spend six months being lost in some forgotten forest? That's a lot of time away from your precious tinned seaweed, you know.'

She looked up at him as he stubbed out the putrid cigar on the arm of the chair. 'All right, all right, all right,' she croaked, 'we go to the Popocatepetl Club.'

'So you see, I've taken everything into account. When you're a genius you tend to. And being a seasoned traveller has taught me that time, that most elusive treasure, is not to be wasted.' He took his gold fob-watch from the pocket of his waistcoat and examined it in the flickering, swinging light of the paraffin lamp above. 'Arrr. Time once again.'

'Time for what? Seaweed?'

'No, bucketbeak. Time to check the inventory.'

'Not again,' whined Desdemona. 'We did it only this morning. It was exactly the same as when we checked it last night. And the night before. And the night before that. Nothing's gone missing——'

'One cannot be too careful. Especially when one is surrounded by deceitful sailors such as these.'

'You should talk,' she thought.

'I wouldn't trust them as far as I could hurl them.'

'Craaark! That'll be the day. You even complain when you have to raise your voice.'

'*What*?' Bone began to lift himself out of the chair, his eyes piercing in the direction of the grottily feathered one. At that moment the ship rocked and swayed. He lowered himself and stroked his bristling beard. 'Antiquity Squad,' he sang softly.

'Craaaaaark!'

'Any more of your insolence and I'll poke you out the porthole. Now get behind the curtain and open the trunk.'

She hopped across the teetering cabin floor and slunk behind the tatty curtain. Bone pulled a dog-eared notepad from his back pocket and began to read in a monotonous rumble:

'Manicure kit in tortoiseshell case?'

'Check,' she replied.

'Fez collection?'

'Check.'

'With and without tassels?'

'With and without.'

'Three pairs of polyester plus-fours?'

'Check.'

'Spotted, plaid and checked?'

'Check spotted, check plaid, check checked.'

'One dozen brand-new unpacked shirts from Port Moresby in the following colours: Bold Purple?'

'Check.'

'Mustard?'

'Check.'

'Brilliant Lemon?'

'Check.'

'Alsatian?'

'Yeergh...check.'

'And one floral—Bougainvillea Design?'

'And one floral, check.'

'Two extra waistcoats, both Emerald Green?'

'Yes,' Desdemona said. 'They're here, along with all your neckties, spats and socks.'

'Compass and sextant?'

'Check.'

'Telescope?'

'Telescope...telescope...check.'

Bone turned the page. 'One antique Ottoman Empire miniature cannon, purloined from the Cairo Museum, to be used in the case of unforeseen obstacles?'

'Like what?'

'I don't know,' the big man grumbled, his stomach churning slightly as the opposite end of the cabin rose up in front of him. 'Butterflies perhaps. I've always wanted to start a collection. Is it there, or have those rude sailors swiped it?'

'It's here.'

'Say ''check''.'

'Check.'

'Assortment of antique Ottoman Empire miniature-cannon cannonballs, also purloined from the Cairo Museum?'

'Check.'

He rubbed his thighs and grimaced. 'I had to go through an extraordinary amount of discomfort to get those without arousing the suspicion of the Guards——'

'Never mind, never mind, never mind, what's one pair of ruined plus-fours in the quest for greatness? Let's get on with it!'

'Hrrmph. Where were we? Arrr. One plate camera with tripod and black silk daylight-cover, purloined from Miss Pyrella Frith* when she wasn't looking?'

'Check.'

'Large box of plastic baubles, to be given as presents to hostile tribes?'

'Check.'

'Large box of tinted photographs of myself, to be given as presents to *extremely* hostile tribes?'

'You may as well be giving them poison for their arrow tips,' thought Desdemona, but in order to get things finished as quickly as possible, she replied in the usual manner. 'Check.'

Bone stood unsteadily and hoisted the curtain aside. He reached into the trunk and, picking out one of the photographs, held it admiringly at arm's length. 'Arrr,'

---

*   The talented archaeological photographer whose services Cairo Jim had employed on more than one occasion.

he sighed. 'Mother used to be enormously fond of this likeness. "What a handsome chap I have," she used to say.'

'What a hammy chap, I would've said,' muttered the raven under her breath.

Bone turned fiercely. *'What did you say?'*

'Clammy map,' she replied quickly, shoving her beak deep into the trunk.

'What?'

'The map of Peru,' came her muffled croak. 'It's got clammy. There's mould up Cuzco way.'

'Hmmmm. There must be water getting into the trunk somewhere. That's the bother with having to charter such a stinky boat as this. When we've finished checking, you'd better locate the leak.' The ship lurched, and Bone fell back into the armchair.

'Come on, come on, let's get this all finished.'

He ran his finger down the list. 'Arr, here we are. My extremely valuable antique wind-up gramophone and collection of Wurlitzer-organ tunes?'

'Check.'

Bone continued to read, relentlessly checking the food provisions item by item, and hoped the larger cargo stored below in the cavernous prunewhiffy hold was secure: his ornate tent-pavilion and the extra-large camel, complete with ploughing apparatus.

'I've been wanting to ask,' Desdemona interrupted at this point, 'what do we need a camel and plough for?'

'Time will reveal all,' he answered mysteriously. 'And now the final item: one silver-plated megaphone with padded handle?'

'It's hanging on the hook above your head.'

'Arr. Of course.'

'What do we need *that* for?'

'Because, foolish fleas, it's an essential part of The Plan.'

'A *megaphone*?'

Bone sighed. 'If I were to go into Peru as Captain Neptune Bone, archaeologist and genius, then when I'd obtained the potion and after I'd melted down the doors of the Cairo Museum and swiped all the gold and become fabulously wealthy, those goody-goody members of the Antiquity Squad might put two and two together——'

'And get five.'

'And get five. *No, you noisome nincompoop*, it might register with them that I had used the potion for this Brilliant Deed.'

'How would they find out?'

'I have learned that one cannot trust anyone except one's own mother. That is why I have the megaphone.'

'I still don't understand.'

'It's my disguise.'

'What? You'll look ridiculous with that on your head. It'll squash your fez.'

'No, gormless, I mean it's part of the *deception*. From the moment we arrive in Peru until the time we leave, I shall be known as Otto von Mostetot, the famous motion-picture director.'

'Never heard of him,' said Desdemona, pecking for a flea.

'Precisely. Nobody has. He doesn't exist. This way,

after the magnificent swindle, no one will be able to trace him.'

'Ah. Now I see.'

'We will tell everyone in Peru that we are looking for the City of ChaCha Muchos in order to make a film about it. The megaphone will add to the masquerade. It will also come in useful as a means of ordering our porter about. I'm sure we'll need one for the few essential items we've just checked.'

'Craaark. You bet. I'm not lugging all that lot.'

Bone ignored her and examined once again his fob-watch. 'Arrr. Will this voyage never end? I think I shall try and get some rest. All of a sudden I'm not feeling my usual self.'

The raven's eyes throbbed gloatingly. 'Seasick, perhaps?'

He snapped the watch cover shut. 'A Bone never gets seasick!'

'You're very green, my Captain.'

'It's all the stuffy air in here. When was the last time you *bathed*?'

'Nevermore.'

'You positively reek.' He stood carefully and stumbled towards the stained hammock, which was swinging back and forth with increasing speed.

'This'll be good,' thought Desdemona.

Captain Neptune Bone paused for a moment, his hands clutching the end of the hammock uncertainly. He would attempt his next movement when the ship was not rolling. When he thought an appropriate calm had settled, he gingerly lifted a leg and placed his knee onto the woven bedding. So far he had made it.

Then all at once, the ship creaked and shot up into the air as it crested an almighty fist of black water. The hammock swivelled and flipped, and Bone went crashing to the floor with a huge *klunk*.

Desdemona laughed so much she had to go outside.

'Aaaar, I think that just for tonight I shall sleep down here,' moaned Neptune Bone, and he nestled into the knot-holed floorboards as the SS *Dark Enterprise* juddered onwards through the roily, swelling depths of the Caribbean Sea.

3

AT THE POPOCATEPETL CLUB

'My goodness,' remarked Cairo Jim, peering up at the sky as he strolled along with his friend, 'look at that colour. You'd hardly think it was night, would you? It's as though the very ceiling of the world has been painted in some wonderful pinkish hue, with little matchlights winking here and there. Or is it more orange? What do you think, Miss Osgood?'

'I think we'd better get a move on if we're to get a table,' Jocelyn said, stepping up her pace.

They walked briskly then, through narrow streets paved with roughly cobbled stones, past darkened houses and small shops lit by dim globes, until they reached a large square with an old, stone fountain in the middle of it. Jocelyn informed Jim that this was the centre of the city of Lima. The Popocatepetl Club was on the other side of the square.

But when they arrived, she pushed her curls back behind her ears and looked puzzled. 'That's odd,' she frowned. 'There're no lights on.' She checked her watch. 'Normally at this hour the place is blazing.'

'Maybe they're closed tonight,' suggested Jim.

'The Popocatepetl Club? Never.' She went to the

double doors and banged hard on the thick wood. They waited in silence as nothing happened. There were no footsteps, no sounds at all. Then, just as she was about to bang again, a small peep-hole no bigger than a playing card slid open with a sharp *clack*.

'Si?' came a voice.

Jocelyn peered through the hole at what appeared to be a mass of dark, thick, tangly hair. 'Hello?'

'Hola?'

'Is that Mendoza?'

'Si,' answered the voice. 'Who is this?'

'Jocelyn Osgood. Are you opening tonight?'

'Hold onto your alpacas, I just fetch a box.' The hair disappeared. There was the sound of footsteps, then a wooden scraping noise, then very quickly a set of eyes popped up and blinked through the hole. 'Ah, Senorita Osgood! So good to see you again. Wait, wait, I unlock for you.'

The peep-hole clacked shut and for nearly a full minute they could hear the sound of keys being tried and jiggled in the lock.

'Is that man new?' whispered Jim. 'He seems to be having some bother.'

'Mendoza? Oh, dear, no. Apparently he's been here for years.' She lowered her voice. 'He's just not very good with locks.'

At last the doors opened and a short, musclebound man with hair that looked like a curly mat ushered them in with a deep bow. 'Come in, come in, it has been such a long time.'

They entered a large, shadowy foyer lined with palm trees planted in chunky terra-cotta pots. On the walls were posters of a tall woman in a bright red dress with frills hanging from the sleeves like fruit from a tree. Jim also spied several small notices, all bearing the warning NO SCOUNDRELS ADMITTED.

'Mendoza, I'd like you to meet my very good friend, Cairo Jim.'

'I am delighted,' Mendoza said, reaching for Jim's hand. 'Any amigo of Senorita Osgood's——' He stopped and gripped Jim's hand extra tightly. 'Tell me one thing,' and he squinted suspiciously, 'are you by any chance an *aristocrat*?' He pronounced the word as though he had just swallowed a cup of castor oil.

'Er, no. I'm an archaeologist as a matter of fact. And I write the occasional po——'

'Then that is okay. Welcome to the Popocatepetl Club.'

'Why is everything in darkness?' Jocelyn asked.

'But it is only just after seven. We do not open until half an hour, you know that, senorita.'

'I make it nearly eight-thirty. How about you, Jim?'

Jim looked at his Cutterscrog. 'Yes, I'm the same.'

Mendoza looked horrified. 'Oh, no, by the Mother Earth, I must have forgotten to wind the clock. Miss del Tempo will be furious with me. Come, come, I find you the best table in the house. Then I go and,' (he took a huge and loud gulp) 'break the news to Miss del Tempo. Follow me, please.' He reached up and adjusted his hair, jerking it sharply across the left side of his head (an action Jim could not help noticing), and led them into the main ballroom. 'Wait here for one momento while I go and turn on the lights.'

This took a little time. There were several sounds of heavy objects being knocked over, and some breaking glass, and a noise like a palm tree falling, and then the ballroom was instantly and brilliantly lit up by an enormous chandelier which hung over them.

'Ah-ha. I knew it was here somewhere.'

Jocelyn and Jim blinked as their eyes adjusted to the light. Gradually the ballroom became easier to see. At the far end of the room there was a large stage arranged with music stands and chairs. In the centre of the stage, propped up against the conductor's stand, was a noticeboard with a big sign in colourful letters:

TONIGHT!
BY SPECIAL ARRANGEMENT!
MISS DOLORES DEL TEMPO
WILL BE ACCOMPANIED BY
PERCY AND HIS PERUVIANS
(SCOUNDRELS NOT ALLOWED)
(UNDER ANY CIRCUMSTANCES)

Below the lettering was a black-and-white photograph of Percy and his Peruvians. They were all holding their instruments proudly and smiling toothy smiles, and they all wore ponchos and hats with long flaps that covered their ears.

Mendoza reappeared rubbing his backside, and took them to a table very close to the stage. He arranged their chairs, and when they were seated, he flicked on a small green lamp in the centre of the table.

He smiled. 'Now,' he said, 'I get you something to drink. Senorita Osgood?'

'I'll have a Kosciusko, please. With lots of papaya juice.'

'Very good. And Senor Cairo?'

'Do you do Belzoni Whoppers?' Jim asked.

'Senor?'

'It's a fruity drink. Very popular at the Old Relics Society in Cairo.'

'I am afraid we do not.'

'Oh.'

'But we do a very good Kilimanjaro. Perhaps the senor would like that? It is *very* fruity.'

'All right. A Kilimanjaro, thank you.'

'Very good.' And off he sped.

Jocelyn looked hard at the photograph of Percy and his Peruvians. 'Hmmm,' she said. 'There's something very familiar about that orchestra.'

Jim removed his pith helmet and placed it on the table. 'Most bands are much the same really, if you ask me,' he said, fiddling with the brim. 'Tell me something, Miss Osgood...'

'Mmm?'

'When we came in, why did that man Mendoza want to know if I were an aristocrat? And what of all those strange signs that say "No Scoundrels"?'

'Ah. Those are his doing. He put them up after the last time Dolores was deceived.'

'Deceived?'

'Yes. It happens all the time. You see, she's mad about royalty or the aristocracy. She'd love to have a title all her own, to be a Duchess or a Baroness or whatever. And there are a lot of chaps about who prey on that to become friends with her. She almost married a Count last year—I was even sent an invitation to the wedding—but he got cold feet at the last minute. That was when they found out he wasn't a Count at all. Only pretending. Turned out he had less royal blood than she did.'

'How rude,' said Cairo Jim.

'Oh, she bounced back. Eventually. She wanted to shoot him with a cannon at first, but she calmed down soon enough when the local museum wouldn't let her have one. It wasn't the first time she'd been tricked. A year before that there was the Italian Prince. *He* turned out to be a telephone wiper.'

'A telephone wiper?'

'Yes, someone who gets paid to go around and clean people's telephones with moist little towelettes. It's supposed to cut down on germs, but all it seems to do is make the handset slippery for a few days.'

'Oh dear.'

'So anyway Mendoza's become quite protective. Won't let anyone near her unless he thinks they're on the level. He can't bear to see her tricked again.' She leaned closer and whispered in Jim's ear, 'Just between you and me, I think he's rather stuck on her.'

'Mmm-hmm?' Jim was glad he had archaeology in his life to keep him busy.

Presently Mendoza returned, bearing their drinks. 'With the compliments of Miss del Tempo,' he said, placing them on the table. 'She apologises that things are running late, and says the show will commence very shortly. Percy's fellows are tuning up in the back room, as a matter of fact. They are a peachy band, let me tell you. Ah, look, people are arriving now, see? Si. Excuse me.' He rushed away to the front doors.

Gradually, as Jocelyn and Jim sipped their drinks, the Popocatepetl Club began to fill with well-dressed people. Most of the men wore smart, dark suits and black bow ties and their shoes were as reflective as mirrors. The women wore long elegant evening frocks, many of which were covered in sparkling sequins. Jim felt a bit out of place in his extra-wide Sahara shorts.

Then Percy and his Peruvians began to take their places on the stage. Jocelyn frowned and bit her lip. She laid her hand on Jim's forearm. 'Don't *you* think there's something a little strange about those musicians?' she asked quietly.

He looked carefully. 'No. They just seem very cheerful, that's all.'

'Look at their eyes.'

'Why, they're all twinkling!'

'No, no, no, look, Jim, they're all *blue*.'

'Well, so are mine for that matter. Both of them.'

'Yes, but for *Peruvians* that's very unusual. Hmmm. You know, I don't think they're from Peru at all. Why, I bet——'

Suddenly the chandelier lights snapped off and a huge, wobbly beam of bright white light appeared centre-stage, followed by a drumroll and a trumpeting *taa-daa*. Into the wobbly light stepped the tallest woman Cairo Jim had ever seen.

'That's Dolores,' Jocelyn whispered.

'Well, I'll be swoggled,' said Jim in a startled sort of way.

Miss Dolores del Tempo stood before them in an effervescent red dress, the same dress they had seen on the posters in the foyer. Clusters of heavy frills fell from her elbows and above her knees in a scallopy formation, so that whenever she moved even slightly they ruffled excitedly. Her hair was glossy black and held back in a bun by two large red combs, and she had an exceedingly strong jaw.

She waited for a moment as the polite applause died down. The bright white light continued to wobble as she stepped up to the microphone and blew into it. This caused a violent symphony of shrill feedback noises to whistle through the ballroom, and everyone put their hands quickly over their ears.

Then the feedback whistled away to nothing and Dolores del Tempo spoke.

'Good evening, senoritas and senors and everyone else. Welcome to the Popocatepetl Club. I would like very much now to sing for you a little tune entitled "Lana the Lovesick Llama", and I would like to dedicate this to my amiga, Senorita Jocelyn Osgood of Valkyrian Airways...'

The wobbly spotlight darted across to the table, illuminating all of Jocelyn and, at the very edge of the circle of light, Cairo Jim's nose.

And something unusual happened: small cries of 'Yah, goodness!', 'Jocelyn Osgood? Wunderbar!' and 'Ah, the Valkyrie of my dreams!' came from Percy's Peruvians, and the clarinettist and trombonist sprang up to get a proper glimpse of her. She was apparently very popular with the rhythm section as well, and they peered over the heads of their fellow musicians to have a good view.

'I should have known,' Jocelyn whispered to Jim. 'Hear those accents? They're not Peruvian at all.'

'I don't under——'

'That's not Percy and his Peruvians,' she said in some alarm. 'That's Terry and his Tyroleans! I had them on a flight some months ago. For some reason they all took a great shine to me. I can't think why, I certainly gave them no encouragement.'

'Hit it, boys,' called Dolores del Tempo, picking up an enormous pair of maracas. The spotlight whizzed wobblingly back to her.

'I bet they're even wearing those little leather shorts under their ponchos,' Jocelyn sniffed.

The Tyrolean–Peruvians could not hear their leader hitting his baton fiercely against the conductor's stand. 'Come on, you fellows,' he hissed, 'sit down and pay attention! Miss del Tempo is ready to commence.'

'She has wonderful eyes,' said Helmut the trombonist dreamily. 'Like a picture, yah, Klaus?'

'She vould be my pin-up, if only I could get a photograph of her,' sighed Klaus who, when he was not dreaming about Jocelyn Osgood, played the melophone better than anyone else in the world.

'I said, *hit it*!'

At Miss del Tempo's powerful shout they promptly sat down, snatching up their instruments.

'Ah, ein, ah, zwei, ah ein zwei drei...' began Terry. Dolores del Tempo began jiggling her frills and shaking her maracas to the melody. Then she began to sing in a clear, strong voice:

In that corner of the world
where maracas are a-shaking,
(cha-cha-cha, cha-cha-cha)
where siestas they are taking,
you may meet on the street
by a sultry hacienda
(cha-cha-cha, cha-cha-cha)
a sweet llama who is tender:

She is loving, she is warm,
she is kissable and crazy,
(cha-cha-cha, cha-cha-cha)
if at times a little lazy,
but the pride and the joy
she is of her dear old mama,
(cha-cha-cha, cha-cha-cha)
this sweet beast whom they call *Lana*.

Now the gentlemen come down
with intentions clear to court her
(cha-cha-cha, cha-cha-cha)
now they offer beer and water,
'Would you like a little fish?'
Then they try a little harder:
(cha-cha-cha, cha-cha-cha)
'Would you like my empanada?'*

But she sits, far removed
on the Podmore Avenida
(cha-cha-cha, cha-cha-cha)
with the gentlemen who feed her,
with the mules passing by
and the clouds above much faster,
(cha-cha-cha, cha-cha-cha)
yearning for her long-lost master.

---

* Meat pie.

He was not a mountaineer,
nor a cobbler nor tailor,
(cha-cha-cha, cha-cha-cha)
he was Keith the burly sailor
with a chest like an ox
and a lot of bright tattoos-o
(cha-cha-cha, cha-cha-cha)
and a voice like E. Caruso.

At this point Terry and his Tyroleans played along merrily while Miss Dolores del Tempo did a jiggling kind of dance, shaking her maracas wildly and flouncing her huge frilly hems and sleeves as though there was no tomorrow. This lively activity appeared to be too much for the spotlight, which now became even *more* wobbly as it whizzed this way and that, trying to illuminate her rhythmic body. Sometimes it threw its beam onto her face, sometimes onto her knees, sometimes onto a section of her body just above her hip, sometimes on only her hair and quite a bit of the back wall, sometimes onto some of Terry's Tyroleans, and once onto an elegant woman in the audience who, much to her husband's embarrassment, happened to be blowing her nose on the tablecloth.

The frienzied, whizzing beam was giving Jim a headache. 'My goodness,' he groaned, 'that spotlight operator seems to be having a bit of strife, wouldn't you say, Miss Osgood?'

'Probably Mendoza,' she nodded. 'He's never been good with spotlights as a rule.'

Then Miss Dolores del Tempo stopped her jiggling and flouncing and shaking and resumed her song:

But Keith sailed far away.
Now she always keeps her eyes on
(cha-cha-cha, cha-cha-cha)
that elusive far horizon
in the hope he'll return
and he'll come and raid the larder
(cha-cha-cha, cha-cha-cha)
and give her his empanada.

Now you've heard the sorry tale
of the llama they call Lana
(cha-cha-cha, cha-cha-cha)
—gosh, I feel like a banana—
burly Keith's far away,
somewhere fishing for piranha,
(cha-cha-cha, cha-cha-cha)
singing: *'I will return*
(cha-cha-cha)
manyana!'
(cha-cha-cha-*cha-cha*!)

A loud sea of applause broke out from all the tables, causing the chandelier to tinkle in a dangerous manner.

Dolores bowed and blew many sloppy kisses to her audience. Then she left Terry and his Tyroleans to their rollicking melodies, and hurtled to the table of Jocelyn and Jim.

'Jocelyn, welcome back!' Dolores bent and kissed her on both cheeks.

Jocelyn smiled. 'It's good to be here. Dolores, I'd like you to meet my very good friend, Cairo Jim.'

Jim stood and shook her hand. 'It's a pleasure to meet you, Miss del Tempo.'

'The pleasure is all mine. Please sit down.' The archaeologist–poet did so, and Dolores took a chair close to Jocelyn. Even when she was seated, it seemed to Jim that she was still standing.

'I like your singing very much, Miss del Tempo,' he said.

'Why, gracias, senor. That is a jaunty pith helmet you have.'

'Thank *you*. I did think, though,' he continued, 'that your spotlight was a little...'

'Si?'

'...trembly.'

'Ah!' said Dolores del Tempo, throwing up her hands, 'that is Mendoza. He works it. The day he gets the sack will not be a day too soon for me, I can tell you. He reckons it goes all over the place like that because I am so tall and he cannot get me lit all at once, so he has to shine a little here and there——'

'Miss del Tempo, you sang so beautifully,' gushed Mendoza, appearing suddenly behind her. 'And your frills moved so *rhythmically*. But I must apologise for the spotlight.'

'Ah, *Mendoza*,' she greeted him as though she had not been *thinking*, let alone *talking* about him. 'Gracias. Why don't you be a good little man and bring us some refreshments?'

'At once, Miss del Tempo, there is nothing else I would rather be doing.' He bowed and raced off, straight into a dancing couple who did not have time to dive out of the way.

Dolores turned back to Jim. 'So tell me, senor, what brings you to Peru?'

Before Jim had a chance to open his mouth, Jocelyn enthusiastically told her the reason. Dolores's large, dark eyes lit up.

'*ChaCha Muchos*?' she gasped. 'You are going to try and find it? Ah!' Her eyes meandered to the mirrored ceiling. 'The Lost City of the Dancers. How exciting! Oh, but you must be so brave, Senor Cairo.'

'You know of it then?' asked Jim, leaning forward and propping his elbows on the top of his pith helmet. 'It may exist after all?'

'As sure as I am a del Tempo it exists! Oh, I have known of it for so long. . .' A strange smile spread across her lips. 'I first heard of this City when I was a small girl, and ever since. . .oh, Senor Cairo, please may I ask a great favour of you?'

'Certainly.'

She reached over and grasped his hands. 'Please would you permit me to come along with you on your search? I would be no trouble, I promise.' She gazed at him with imploring, pleading eyebrows.

'I'm sure Jim will have enough to worry about by himself,' Jocelyn advised firmly, separating their hands. 'And anyway Dolores, the jungle is no place for frills and maracas.'

'I'm afraid Miss Osgood is right, Miss del Tempo. Much as I'd like to say yes, it's entirely out of the question.'

'Really? Are you quite, quite sure, senor?'

'Quite sure,' he nodded.

'I understand,' frowned Dolores.

'Miss del Tempo, there are many things I need to know, and that's why we've come to you. Miss

Osgood speaks very highly of you as being an expert on Peruvian history.'

This compliment made Dolores forget her disappointment for the time being, and she straightened in her chair and ran both hands across her sleek hairdo. 'Ask away, senor,' she said, blinking her thick eyelashes in what she imagined was the manner of someone who was an expert on Peruvian history. 'I will help you as much as my knowledge allows.'

'By any chance do you know what actually became of the people of ChaCha Muchos? Is it possible they still exist?'

'That, nobody knows for certain. It is said in old Peruvian legends that after they had built their City, they did nothing but dance. On and on and on, night and day. Under the hides of them there was such a hunger to dance that they could do nothing else. This is what led to their downfall. According to the legends, *the entire civilisation danced itself to extinction.*'

'How melancholy,' said Jocelyn Osgood.

'Exactly.' Dolores smiled and lowered her voice to a secretive tone. 'It is also said that ChaCha Muchos was the place where they invented most of the dances we dance today: the rumba, the samba, the tango and fandango, even the foxtrot and the Emnobellian Whoopskick Polka, all of them came from this sad but richly cultured place.'

'How were they handed down?' Jocelyn wondered.

'Possibly by explorers and traders,' said Dolores. 'They may have come into contact with a local tribe, who in turn may have had earlier contact with the ChaCha Muchonians. This tribe may have taught the explorers and traders the dances, and the explorers and traders may have taken them back to their own countries. That may be how so many of the dances have spread throughout the world.'

'Ah,' said Cairo Jim, stroking his chin.

'Jim was wondering if you might be able to point him in the right direction,' Jocelyn said.

'Yes,' nodded Jim, pulling out his map of Peru from inside his shirt and unfolding it on the table. He ran his finger in a widish circle over the area north of Cuzco. 'This is where I think it might be, but I'm only going on an engraving from a very old, dusty book.'

Dolores leaned forward, her eyes wider and darker than before. 'I can tell you where to look,' she said, her voice like moonbeam-shimmer. She reached across and pointed with her long, red-fingernailed digit.

Cairo Jim and Jocelyn Osgood bent their heads low over the map. 'HokeyCokey Mountain,' read Jim aloud. 'Of course! Why didn't I see it before?' He made a quick measure of the scaled distance. 'About two hundred and fifty kilometres or so from Cuzco as the Egyptian vulture flies...and look, there's something written near the mountain!' He squinted hard, then read out: ' "Unexplored Territory. Possibly Uninhabited. Possibly Not." Hmmm.' He ran his index finger over his top lip.

'Anything wrong, Jim?'

'No, Miss Osgood. Not really. I'm just wondering how I'm to get out there. As you see, the road stops well before HokeyCokey begins.'

'Ah,' said Dolores, 'there are no roads leading into

the *cloudforest*. That is where you must travel first. The mountain will rise out of this misty place.'

'The cloudforest, you say?' said Jim.

'There may not be any roads,' said Jocelyn, smiling, 'but there is *sky*.' Jim looked at her. 'Well, don't look so surprised,' she said. 'It's about time I did some *real* flying again. One gets tired of being a Flight Attendant *all* the time. Would you like a ride?'

Cairo Jim's excitement rose up through his chest, all the way up into the poetry cells of his brain. Before he knew it, he was blurting:

Is the Sphinx a piece of sculpture?
Is an obelisk tall and straight?
Do feluccas sail upon the Nile from early morn till late?
Was Rameses a mighty King?
Was Hatshepsut a Queen?
Was Cleopatra's library the greatest ever seen?
Do the famed Memnon Colossi
both weigh more than half a ton?
Does the pyramid of Chephren rise on up to meet the
    sun?

'A simple "yes" would've done the trick,' winced Jocelyn.

'You bet your flying goggles. Are you sure you don't mind?'

'Of course not. I have a few days off anyway. They have to give us time between flights, otherwise we get tired and drop things.' She leaned back and folded her arms. 'So it's settled then. I think we should leave early tomorrow morning. Does that suit?'

'Certainly,' answered Jim.

'I know where I can hire a good little Tiger Moth with plenty of room for——'

'Senor, are you sure you could not find room for *me*?' Dolores fluttered her eyelashes. 'Please reconsider. I assure you, I would be no nuisance.'

'I'm very sorry, Miss del Tempo, especially after all the help you've been tonight, but——'

'*Aaaaaarrrgggghhh!*' shouted Jocelyn, jumping out of her chair, the back of her evening frock drenched and sopping from the trayful of drinks Mendoza had just spilled down it.

Miss Dolores del Tempo leapt to her feet, and all the Furies seemed to break loose from her heavily crimsoned lips as she began to rouse on the unfortunate man. She yelled and yelled into his face, and in between yelling she apologised to Jocelyn and began to mop the dripping dress with Mendoza's necktie which she yanked from under his collar.

Mendoza also apologised in a choking sort of way and then made things worse as he tried to assist by using the tablecloth from the next table. This resulted in five very large plates of jellied-eel-flavoured blancmange (which the people at that table were about to start eating) as well as five large Krakatoas (which they had only just started drinking) spilling onto the floor around Mendoza's feet.

The noise of the crashing glass and sloshing blancmange made Klaus and Helmut lose their places in the tune they were playing, and one of the other Tyroleans then lost his patience with them, so he turned around and did something rude with his tongue and fingers, and both Klaus and Helmut did something rude back to him by blowing their melophone and trombone loudly into each of his ears, an action which set the xylophonists off into a nasty musical battle with the violinists (who always took Klaus's and Helmut's side in matters like this), much to the complete dismay of Terry who was now almost snapping his wrist in half as he furiously struck his conductor's stand with his baton, trying to gain control of his fellows once again and get them to play something which didn't sound like a battalion of tomcats out to break the sound barrier.

And through it all Dolores kept rousing and yelling at Mendoza, her voice making the chandelier tremble.

But, as sometimes happens in the face of catastrophe, everything turned out all right in the end; it gave Jocelyn and Jim the chance to leave early (much to the dismay of Terry's Tyroleans, who were all hoping for a dance), before Dolores del Tempo's violin solo. That, as anyone who has visited the Popocatepetl Club knows, is a thing to be avoided at all costs.

The tall woman played with extra gusto that evening, ignoring the crowds rushing to get their hats and coats from the cloakroom, for she was angry. Angry that she had missed the opportunity to be part of the search for the City of ChaCha Muchos. For her own reasons it was a thing she wanted desperately, and as she sawed away at the violin with her bow, she resolved that if the opportunity ever arose again she would do all within her power not to let it slip from her grasp.

4

JOCELYN AT THE JOYSTICK

THE next afternoon Jocelyn Osgood gave the propeller of the rented Tiger Moth a decidedly good jerk and it spluttered to life with a ferocious roar.

She quickly fastened her flying helmet, pulled her goggles down over her eyes, and leapt swiftly into the cockpit, beside Cairo Jim. 'You'd better put your chinstrap down,' she shouted.

'Good idea,' he shouted back, pulling it down from the brim of his helmet and fixing it firmly under his chin.

Jocelyn stepped on the gas. The aircraft began to trundle down the runway of the Lima Grand Splendid Aerodrome and before Jim could say 'Nespernub' they were up and away.

It was a clear, sunny sky into which they roared. Jocelyn guided them low over the city for a few minutes before accelerating higher into the cloudless blue firmament. Then she turned sharply to the south, and Lima shrank smaller and smaller, moment by moment. At last the pattern of dots which was the huge city disappeared completely from view.

'Miss Osgood,' Jim yelled, his brow lined with puzzlement, 'I don't want to seem rude, but aren't we flying in the wrong direction?'

Jocelyn smiled. 'Are we?' she shouted back.

'I'd say so. According to my map, Cuzco is east of Lima. The instruments on your control panel indicate we're heading *south*.'

Jocelyn continued to stare directly in front. 'Don't worry,' she hollered. 'We won't get lost. There's something I want to show you.'

'What?'

'Wait and see!' And that was all he was going to get out of her for the time being.

She said nothing more for nearly half an hour, at which time, all at once and without warning, she raised her right wing tip and took the plane sharply down over the wide open stony space beneath them.

'Look!' she shouted excitedly. 'Have you heard of these?'

Jim held on tightly to the side of the plane as he craned his head out to view the scene. Suddenly he gasped.

'Oh, Miss Osgood, how marvellous!'

'I thought you'd be pleased.'

'The famous Lines of Nazca! I never dreamed I'd see them in real life! Oh, whacko!'

As far as the eye could see the desert below was cut with furrowed trenches, all in the forms of simple yet astounding patterns. Each of them was gargantuan and even though he had seen photographs and drawings of them in books, Jim never imagined they would be as walloping as this. Jocelyn lowered the speed of the aircraft and slowly, almost reverently, they flew over each and every shape.

There was an enormous monkey, finely etched deep into the earth, his long tail curling all around him as he lay basking on his gritty patch. Nearby a gigantic hummingbird with a long, thin beak and long, thin tail feathers seemed to hover on the ground, and next to that a monstrous spider whose legs were mightily menacing was weaving a web of intricate and precise beauty. There was also a dog with a tremendous snout and tail, a slithery lizard, a tree with branches stretched and far-reaching, and a huge pair of human hands with spindly fingers that looked like runways at an airport.

'Of all the wonders under the sun,' Jim bellowed. 'Do you know, Miss Osgood, that some archaeologists believe these figures were deliberately dug into the ground by the Ayacucho people for the entertainment of the wealthy classes over thirteen hundred years ago?'

'You don't say?' Jocelyn could see her friend was happy and this made her fly in huge, lazy circles over the ditches and troughs.

'See those scorched patches of earth?'

She peered through her goggles and nodded.

'Well, archaeologists believe those are the spots where the wealthy people launched their hot-air balloons.'

'Pull the other one.'

'No, truly. They used to sail above these patterns so they could see them to their full advantage. Much the same as we're doing now. From the ground they only look like ploughed fields.'

'Hot-air balloons?'

'There are ancient pieces of local pottery and tapestries that show hot-air balloons. They did have them in those days.'

'How about that?'

'I've also read of farmers around here who tell stories of flying people long ago, long before aeroplanes were invented. Some folk think the lines were made by flying saucers or beings from other worlds, but that's all a bit far-fetched, don't you think?'

'I wonder. Heavens, look at the time. I'd better get you off.'

And she about-turned and pointed the propeller towards the low-hanging sun.

Eventually they approached the towering Andes mountains with their white, icy peaks spearing into the clouds. The Tiger Moth threaded its way between these snow-capped giants like a minute fly buzzing in a series of straight lines broken by sharp turns. Soon, in a valley nestled between the bases of several mountains, a sea of pale brown tiles came into view. The dense array of rooftops was broken only by the occasional plaza dotted with greenery and a fountain in the centre.

'Cuzco,' hollered Jocelyn.

'Ah-ha,' shouted Jim. 'Not far now!'

She tilted the left wing downwards and accelerated smartly, and they veered abruptly away from the mountains. The sky ahead was gathering in the dusk and, with every kilometre that blurred away beneath them, Cairo Jim's heart beat faster as he thought of the delicious uncertainty which lay ahead.

*   *   *

'Miss del Tempo,' grovelled Neptune Bone as he sat wedged into the tiny chair at a table in the Popocatepetl Club, 'your very name thrusts sweet bursts of melody into my eardrums.'

'How kind you are, Senor. . .?'

'Mostetot. Otto von Mostetot. But you may call me Otto.'

'That is a fetching fez you are wearing.'

'Thank you.'

'The rakish angle reminds me of—*aaarrrgghhh*!' The tallest woman in Lima leapt from her chair.

'What on earth——?' started Bone, also rising.

'Something down there,' she gasped, pointing under the table. 'Something got me!'

Bone rolled his eyes and bent over. 'You stupid thing,' he hissed at something underneath the tablecloth. 'Get out here at once!'

Desdemona hopped out and up onto the table, where she gobbled at a flea on her wing.

'What do you think you're playing at?' growled Bone.

'I couldn't help myself,' she rasped fiendishly. 'I just came over. . .peckish. . .all of a sudden.'

'What is *this*?' Dolores went grey.

'Ah, Senorita, permit me to introduce my assistant.'

'A *crow*?'

Desdemona shot a glare at her, then at Bone. 'What does she mean, *crow*?'

'Shut your beak,' he snarled whisperingly. 'If she thinks you're a crow, you're a crow.'

'How demeaning. Craaark!'

Bone picked up his megaphone and capped it briskly down on the table so she was trapped beneath it. 'Yes,' he said, turning once again to Dolores. 'A crow is a very handy thing to have as an assistant. Especially when the script calls for rainy scenes. I get her to fly around and spit water onto the actors. It almost looks like the real thing, you understand.'

'I do not understand,' frowned Dolores.

'What? Arr, how remiss of me. I forgot to tell you. I, madam, am a director.'

'A director?'

'A director of motion pictures.'

'Oh, si?'

'Yes.' He stroked his beard out to a fine point and gave her a lopsided smile. 'That great flickering cosmos, that world without end, that celluloid realm of dreams...' He wiggled his eyebrows up and down.

'Why is it I have never heard of you?'

He stopped wiggling and fixed her with a stare she could not contradict. 'I am very big in Sweden,' he boasted.

'You're very big all over the place,' squawked the megaphone. Bone rapped it with his knuckles and a louder squawk shot out as it reverberated like a bell.

'I am here,' he continued, 'on a matter of cinematographical importance. I am looking for a location for a magnificent epic film I intend to make.'

'Oh, si?'

'Yes, a monumental story. I shall write it, direct it, produce it, edit it, compose the music, work the camera and design the frocks. Who knows, I may even make a small appearance in three or four scenes.'

'What will it be about?'

Bone leaned across the table and lowered his voice to a whispering rumble. 'An ancient city,' he said, and smirked.

'An ancient city?' Dolores smirked back at him.

'An ancient city where they danced long ago.'

The eyes of Dolores del Tempo narrowed and then widened, her dark pupils growing bigger and bigger. She took a deep breath. 'I know of such a city, senor.'

'You *do*?' Bone leaned further across the table until his chest was rammed firmly against its edge. He hunched his shoulders in mock amazement. 'You mean that such a city may actually exist? That there is, in this real world, a location the likes of this?'

'You bet your megaphone.'

'Oh, Miss del Tempo, is it at all possible that you may be aware of its location?'

Dolores leaned back, crossed her arms, and smiled mysteriously.

'Oh, come, senorita, I have a feeling you're not telling me everything...'

'Maybe I am, maybe I'm not.'

Bone leaned back and cracked his knuckles loudly.

'Raaaaaark!' echoed Desdemona, whose eyes always throbbed harder and redder whenever he did that.

'Madam, I do not have a moment to waste. My time here is very precious. Here is what I will do: if you can tell me where to find this city, I will give you this.' He reached into the pocket of his plus-fours and took out a wad of money tied tightly by a piece of lavender-coloured twine. 'One thousand Egyptian pounds,' he proclaimed. 'In unmarked notes.'

Dolores threw back her head and laughed loudly, causing the chandelier to dance and tinkle. Then she stopped and looked Bone in the eye. 'Senor von Mostetot——'

'Otto, please.'

'Senor von Mostetot, I have no need and no desire for your money. I earn more than enough here at the Popocatepetl Club.'

'What *can* I give you then?'

'There is nothing I want from you, unless perchance you have a title. You are not a Viscount or an Earl, are you?'

'No, no, no,' scowled Bone. 'Some little man with wonky hair asked me that when I came in.'

'Oh.'

'Madam, I beseech you. Please tell me where I should look. It is of the most excruciating importance to me.'

Dolores knew he was desperate and she knew she had the upper hand. 'I'll do better than that,' she said. 'I will take you there, senor.'

'What?'

'I will come along on your expedition with you. That is the only way you will find the City.'

'Preposterous!' snorted the bearded man.

'Craaaark!' squawked the megaphone.

'Preposterous?'

'Absolutely. I've never heard anything more patently ridiculous in all my days.'

Dolores stood abruptly. 'Well in that case, senor, the little man with the. . .what did you say. . .winky hair will show you to the door. Mendoza!'

Mendoza flung himself out of the dimly lit spaces behind the palm trees and up to her table. 'Si, Miss del Tempo?'

'Senor von Mostetot and his crow——'

'Craaark!'

'——are leaving. Would you escort them?'

'With much delight, Miss del Tempo.' He grabbed Bone by the lapels of his waistcoat and lifted him easily, up and out of his chair.

'Unhand me, you little spider!'

'Good evening, senor.' Dolores began to walk away.

'Stop!' yelled Bone. 'I reconsider!'

She turned her head and regarded him over her shoulder. 'You mean I *am* coming with you?'

'Mmm,' Bone mmmed sullenly.

'Let him go, Mendoza.'

'Si, Miss del Tempo.'

Bone smoothed down his lapels and leaned across the table. 'But I have one condition. . .'

'What?' snapped Dolores, turning to face him.

'That we also take your friend here.'

'Mendoza?'

'Me?' blinked Mendoza. 'Take me where?'

'Yes, Miss del Tempo,' said Bone. 'I have need of someone with his strength. There are a few little pieces of equipment he can carry.'

Dolores put her hands on the table and leaned across it until her nose was within centimetres of Bone's. She could smell prunes on his clothes. 'You mean you want him to be a porter?'

'A porter?' repeated Mendoza. 'For what? Where are we going?'

'If this is to be the case, I too have one condition,' Dolores said. 'He will also carry things for *me*.'

'Such as?' Bone asked.

'Not much.' She stood back to avoid the prune stench. 'Merely some clothes and shoes and feather boas and makeup and looking glasses and the latest edition of *Who's Who* and my manicure kit——'

'Arrr,' nodded Bone approvingly.

'——and hair lotion and barbells and other assorted gymnasium equipment and...oh, yes, of course, my violin. I can't go anywhere without *that*.'

'A porter?' Mendoza said again. 'But where are we going?'

'All right,' Bone grumbled.

'Craaaaaaaark!'

'Be quiet, you megaphoned monstrosity!'

'Good,' smiled Dolores. 'I'm glad that's settled. I think we will travel very well together, Senor von Mostetot.'

'Hrrmph,' hrrmphed Bone.

'And now I think we should have a celebratory juice concoction. Mendoza, bring the senor and myself two large Kahuzis.'

'Certainly.' Mendoza bowed. 'But, please, Miss del Tempo, *where are we going*?'

'To ChaCha Muchos,' sang the towering woman, her eyes gleaming.

'ChaCha Muchos? Peachy!' exclaimed Mendoza. He adjusted his hair and dashed off.

'ChaCha Muchos,' purred Neptune Bone as though it was the first time in his life he had heard it. 'What a wonderful name. What a wonderful, wonderful name. Oh, what a wonderful film I shall make...aaaarrrr...' He closed his eyes and conjured up the doors of the Cairo Museum.

'*Craaaaaaaaaaaarrrrrrkkkk!*' squawked the megaphone.

*　　*　　*

Below the Tiger Moth the cloudforest was dripping with greenery. There was still enough light for Jim and Jocelyn to see the massive vines and lush palms and colossal ferns and trees that lined the muddy brown river. Jim had hoped he might have been able to spy a trail, or better still some kind of building or mound of stones, which may have given a clue as to which direction he should take once he was on ground. But now, looking down on it all, he knew it was merely a dismal hope; everything was too dense. The only way he would find anything would be amidst the undergrowth.

'There it is,' Jocelyn sang out, looking straight ahead at a towering black mass shrouded by the heavy gloaming.

'HokeyCokey,' said Jim. 'And so the trail begins...'

Jocelyn smiled and dipped the right wing. She swerved to avoid flying into a sunset-seeking flock of brilliant yellow and blue macaws, and then started to look for a spot where she could drop Cairo Jim and all his equipment.

INTERLUDE

IT was hot here, prickly and stickily hot, even under
the heavy canopy of flowers and sweeping green
vines that stopped the sunlight from reaching the
watermelon-leafed plants growing on the muddy forest
floor. The air was tight with steam, vapour rising in
thin shafts of fine, wet droplets, and the more the
Indians breathed, the steamier it became.

It was lunchtime for them now, time for them to
rest and eat before proceeding further up the mountain.
Zapateado put down his sleeping bundle where it was
not too muddy, where the small vines and plants were
lush and dense. He sat and wiped his brow with the
back of his smooth hand. It is good to rest, he thought
with a sigh, especially when the forest is so sweltering
and when there is such a long way to go before the
City. He closed his eyes and let his hand drop to his
side, where the small leather pouch hung from his belt.

He heard the sounds of monkeys rustling branches
high above, and then the shattering screeches of the
macaws who had been disturbed by the monkeys'
chattering. Other, closer sounds came to his ears: some
of the smaller children were dancing through the
tangled vines, chanting in their sing-song voices words

that had been passed down through many generations of the tribe. He opened his eyes and beheld their little wrinkled faces damp with heat as they skipped and stepped and strutted through the foliage. Ah, the pleasures of the foxtrot, he thought contentedly.

Then a voice sounded very close to his ear. It did not identify itself, but there was no need for it to; Zapateado could tell whose voice it was by the high-pitched excitement propelling it like wings on a bird.

'Will you tell me something more?' asked the voice.

'What do you wish to be told?' asked Zapateado.

'Tell me what became of Sandra Panza. Tell me how she became Sandra of the Heavens.'

'What happened to her was meant to be,' answered Zapateado. 'It was meant to happen in the same way your loss of wrinkles and white hair is meant to happen, Yupichu. It was the way of the Mother Earth.'

'But why? How?'

'That is a story which needs some understanding. Listen to me carefully.'

The boy sat and hugged his knees, giving the dark-haired man his full attention.

'Long ago,' began Zapateado, his voice rippling as he began to recall the story exactly as it had been told to him by his father, 'in the days before explosions and guns came to this place, the dancing people from Cuzco stumbled through the forest, trying to escape from the Spanish conquistadors. The Cuzconians were in a desperate state, having danced for many days and nights amidst the sharp thorns and spiny roots. When our forefolk came upon them they were exhausted and their ankles badly swollen. They were much in need of attention and so our tribe led them to our village, in those days located at the base of the mountain known as HokeyCokey, which is ancientspeak for "Place of Light Fantastic". Here they stayed for many days, all the while dancing, but only in a gentle manner so that their ankles gradually began to lose their swelling. The people, you see, were unable to stop dancing.'

'Why was this?' the boy asked.

'That is exactly what our tribe wondered as they watched the Cuzconians gambolling around the village, in and out through the trees and plants growing at the edge of the clearing. It was voted that the oldest member of the tribe should ask the Cuzconians why they were unable to cease this reckless behaviour, and so my ancestor Arturo Murrayo was given the task. Warily he approached a woman he had been observing, a woman who stood head and shoulders and head and shoulders again above the other Dancers. She seemed to have some kind of power over them as she directed their movements, and Arturo felt she must be their leader. She was Sandra Panza, the one who had led the rebels away from Cuzco. She was also the maker of a flavoursome treat known as the Cuzco Clackersmacker.

'Arturo Murrayo stood before her, looking up into her dark eyes as she watched the Dancers. There was something in her face that made him hesitate, something that made him go all trembly, a thing most out of character for Arturo Murrayo who was known amongst the tribe for his graceful co-ordination. But he swallowed hard and then asked her: "Why do your people dance so much?"

'Sandra Panza's eyes became darker as she stared at him from her great height. She smiled in a way Arturo had never seen. There was something behind her smile that he could not explain, some kind of secret knowledge there. His heart pulsated with desire to know what this secret knowledge was.

'She answered him in a voice mellow and knowing. "We dance," she said, "because it is within us. It *burns* within us like a fire that can never be extinguished. On and on and on it burns. It is inextinguishable! Feel!" She took the hand of my ancestor and placed it on her forehead. Arturo had to stand on his toes, and he was a very tall man. "Feel the heat of our passion," she commanded.

'The warmth from her forehead filled his hand. It spread down his arm, into his chest, down his backbone, through his entire trunk and filled both his legs right down to his ankles until finally it reached his feet, where it tingled and zinged. Before he knew what was happening, he was tapping his toes to the rhythm of the Cuzconian rebels.

'When the rest of Arturo's tribe saw this, they were puzzled. "What is happening to you?" they asked. Some reached out and touched the old man. Gradually his warmth spread to those nearest him, and then others came and took hold of their hands, attaching themselves in a long chain so they too could be touched by this mysterious power. And *their* feet began to tingle and they, too, shook them to try to get rid of the sensation. They moved forwards and shook, and backwards and shook, and forwards again, and they shook their feet all about. In this way, Yupichu, the line of the Conga was born.

'To the great delight of the Cuzconians, many of our tribe enjoyed this newly discovered activity. For a month the Indians and Cuzconians mingled with each other, the Cuzconians teaching our people many of their oscillations and a few high-kicks for good measure. Then one day Sandra Panza told Arturo Murrayo that it was time for her Dancers to move on. They had been in the same spot for too long, she told him, and there was a danger the Spanish conquistadors would find them. Arturo asked her where they would go and sadly, almost helplessly, she shook her head. "I do not know," she answered. "We will find somewhere else, maybe in the forest, maybe not in the forest. We will remain there for a short time, but then we must move on again. Those conquistadors would be merciless if they were ever to catch us." She let out a huge shudder of a sigh, and Arturo Murrayo could not help thinking how short the tall woman appeared through her despair.

'Then he had an idea. He remembered a place above them, at the very pinnacle of HokeyCokey which, because of its leafy aspect and the surrounding towering cliffs, was undetectable from the base of the mountain and from the bottom of the cloudforested valley. "It would be the perfect place for your people to dwell," he told her excitedly. "They would never have to leave it. Nobody who did not know of it would ever be able to find it! My people would be glad to lead your people there.

It would be the least we could do after the cracking secrets you have shared with us.''

'When she heard this, Sandra Panza straightened, and in an instant appeared taller than she had ever appeared. It was as though her thick, dark hair was brushing the clouds. She reached out and threw her arms around Arturo Murrayo, grasping him so tightly his ears popped. With a gleam in her dark eyes she accepted his offer.

'Early the next morning, before the Fantastic Light had made the side of the mountain bright, the two groups set off along the trail we ourselves are following. It took them a long time to reach the pinnacle because the Cuzconians insisted on stopping at regular intervals to hula and polka, but eventually, after many days of trekking and twostepping, they arrived at the rocky top of HokeyCokey.'

'And here they built the City.'

'Yes, Yupichu. Sandra Panza was pleased with the location, and she was even more pleased with the assistance Arturo could give her in the building process. The Cuzconian rebels, you see, did not have the time or the strength or the inclination to chisel out the thick rock face of the cliffs. They were only interested in dancing; nothing else mattered. When Arturo produced the gourds containing our tribe's inherited wealth—the thick substance which had up until then never been seen by people who were not members of the tribe—Sandra asked him to put it to use on the rocks. Arturo and several other Indians did so, and in little more than seven days they had etched a many-dwellinged City into the harsh walls. Sandra Panza saw the finished City with its laneways and houses and ballrooms and dancing arenas, and she was consumed with pleasure. "You have saved us," she said to Arturo. "You have saved my people and you have given us a place to dwell. In honour of your tribe I shall call our new home 'ChaCha Muchos', and from this day on we shall be known as ChaCha Muchonians. We will wear our name with pride and rhythm, and we will still be dancing on that day when Time and the Horizon become One.''"

Zapateado paused and, his eyes bright, wiped his wet neck with the back of his hand.

'But you have not answered me,' said Yupichu impatiently. 'How did Sandra Panza become Heavenly?'

Zapateado smiled. 'That is the next turn of the tale. After the City was completed it was time for Arturo Murrayo and the Indians to return to the cloudforest where the hunting time was about to begin. Arturo bade his farewells and, leaving some Indians who wished to remain and become Dancers, he took the rest of his tribe down, away from the pinnacle. They would return after the rains had come and when the hunting time was over, Arturo having promised they would bring food to the ChaCha Muchonians. On the way down, they used the potion to melt a special gate into the side of the cliff. This they called "The Moongate", and from it they could see the City high above.

'The rains came and the hunting was done. Six months after they had left, Arturo and several others, laden with salted meats and sacks full of fruit from

the cloudforest, traversed the trail, now made slippery
and muddy from the rains. It took a long time because
of the dangerous state of the jungle. They had to be
ever-aware of falling branches and the lethal Hokey-
Cokey Dancing Tarantula and unexpected rockslides
from the top of the mountain. But finally they arrived
at the pinnacle. And a terrible thing greeted them.'

'What? What?'

'The beautiful City they had left was quiet, empty,
utterly deserted. There were no Dancers, no sounds
of music echoing through the streets or laneways, not
even the chatter of monkeys or the squawks of toucans
in the surrounding trees. Everywhere was ab-so-lute-
ly *still*. It was as though human beings had never been
there at all.

'Arturo and his friends wandered through the
emptiness, searching in vain for any signs of life or
activity. They found nothing but overturned gourds
which had once contained water but were now as dry
as the sand from a dead riverbed. The leaf and twig
sleeping cots which the tribe had made for the Dancers
had fallen apart and were now brittle and crumbly.
Roofs had collapsed, tables had rotted and splintered,
great patches of moss clung to the walls. It looked as
though the City had been deserted for some time,
because already the jungle was starting to reclaim its
territory, with thick, creeping vines and small, eager
plants snaking and thrusting their way between the
walls of rock.

'As Arturo stood in the middle of the silence he
heard a sudden rustling in the ferns behind him. He
turned quickly, silently, his spear at the ready, and

advanced. With a graceful thrust of his weapon he pulled the ferns apart and there, cowering below, was one of the Indians he had left behind with the Dancers. Her eyes were wide with fear and she trembled as though with fever. When she recognised Arturo Murrayo she threw her arms around his legs and wailed loudly. Her cries penetrated the heavy quiet and the friends of Arturo came rushing to see what was wrong. Together they dragged her from the undergrowth and settled her with reassuring words in her native dialect. When she was calm she began to tell them the dreadful things that had happened.

'She told them that after the Indians had returned to the cloudforested hunting grounds the ChaCha Muchonians had continued to dance constantly, without tiring. Twisting hither and thither, skipping and swaying, shimmying and shaking. They would not stop to fetch water or find fruit or hunt the wild Peruvian boar. All they had to eat were the Clackersmackers, now named the ChaCha Clacker-smackers, which Sandra Panza continued to make in the large cauldron our ancestors had carried up for her. But these, delectable as they were, were not enough to satisfy dancing stomachs. The ChaCha Muchonians became hungry and gradually weaker. As the months went by, Sandra Panza watched what was happening and became worried. She tried to dissuade her Dancers from dancing during every waking minute of their days, and suggested they should devote some time to maintaining their city and hunting. But obsession is an obstinate thing, Yupichu, and it was no use. They continued to dance, and the fires within them burnt higher and higher.

'Sandra Panza despaired as every attempt she made to change their behaviour proved useless. All they did was eat Clackersmackers and dance. Then one night, as the moon rose above the Moongate, Sandra was seized by a vision. Her eyes became very, very small, two black dots in a great sea of whiteness. Her limbs moved jerkily, and she began speaking in a loud voice to something no-one else could see, something that seemed to hover somewhere far out in the skies. This something seemed to be beckoning, for she began to nod and walk towards the battlements at the highest edge of the City. "I am coming, I am coming," she was saying in a voice as flat as a river pebble. "I will join you now."

'For the first time since they had arrived at ChaCha Muchos the Dancers stopped dancing and watched their leader, all of them dumbstruck. They followed her through lanes and up paths, climbing higher and higher and far away higher, until she reached the tallest battlement above the raging Marjangower River. There she turned to her people. Standing on the rocky wall in the strong, icy moonlight, she was now the tallest woman ever. She looked down at them and laughed maniacally, and her laughter rang in the ears and clutched at the stomachs of everyone present. No-one could move; they were all stunned by her wild state.

'Then she turned and stretched her arms towards the stars and the moon and the blackness of the heavens. "I am coming," she said, quietly, sadly, hopelessly. She threw a handful of Clackersmackers over her shoulder to the Dancers and with a bold high kick stepped off the battlements and plummeted into eternity.'

Yupichu gave a long whistle.

'Nobody ever saw her again,' continued Zapateado, his voice softer now. 'With her departure the entire City became a place of heavy mourning. The Dancers kept on dancing, slowly, slowly, ever so slowly for Sandra Panza. They did nothing else and gradually their fires began to flicker and dwindle. When these fires were completely dead the people stopped dancing and found themselves quite shockingly helpless. They were unable to do even the simplest tasks such as collecting food or drawing water. And so they got tired, deathly tired, and very sick. Thus it came, Yupichu, that the ChaCha Muchonians were no more...

'Arturo Murrayo and his friends took the woman who had told them this story back down to the cloudforest where she soon settled back into the Indians' society. And shortly after, Arturo had a dream. It was so strong and real that for several days after, he did not believe he was actually awake, but was convinced he was dreaming *then*. In his dream he saw Sandra Panza returning to the City from her great height, bringing her music with her, looking down upon him. Afterwards he told the others she had stood before him saying, "Arturo, do not despair. I shall return. I shall return to the City you have built for us and then we shall build a *new* civilisation, a dancing society of great happiness and rhythm and little trouble. Wait for me, Arturo Murrayo. Bring your people to the top of HokeyCokey every year during the rains until I come back with my music...let there be no mournful refrains. . .wait for me in hope, for I shall return." And then she faded away into a cloud of fine, grey mist.'

Zapateado licked his lips. He smiled gently and nodded his head. 'That is how we have Sandra of the Heavens. That is why we wait. That is why we go now to the City.'

He stood and, taking a deep breath, stretched first one leg and then the other in an admirable arabesque. Then he picked up his sleeping bundle and began to make his way out of the clearing, the tribe following him up the hill in small, dawdling groups.

Yupichu stayed where he was. His head was spinning with the enormity of the tale which now, at last, he knew. And knowing it, something curious started happening inside him. Somewhere in his brain all kinds of thoughts which had lain very still for a long time began to form into a pattern of ideas which all at once excited and overwhelmed him. He thought the pattern of ideas through until they became a plan, a plan as real and as strong as his arm.

He stood and brushed away a lock of greyish hair from his eyes. He was ripened now, a grown-up, and he vowed to do something to prove it to the rest of the tribe. Something nobody else had done in the last five hundred years. His solar plexus was glowing and his heart was pounding rapidly.

He would find their Sandra of the Heavens, and *he* would lead Her back to Her people in such a triumphant dance that the jungle would still be babbling about it five hundred years from now. . .

5

INTO THE CLOUDFOREST

Cairo Jim liked to travel as lightly as possible when on an expedition. Inside his leather knapsack he carried the large green book from the Old Relics Society library; his map of Peru; a sturdy torch; one set of spare torch batteries; his water bottle filled with fresh water; a small jar of water-purification tablets; three boxes of waterproof matches; four tins of preserved food in case there was no fresh fruit available; his pocket knife which had a tin opener, small saw, pair of scissors, magnifying glass, knife, spoon, fork and a very sharp thing ideal for getting small furry berries out of the soles of his boots; an enamel mug and plate; tea and sugar; his pencil case with some pens and pencils in it; his journal; a bottle of insect repellent; a bottle of sunscreen lotion; toothbrush, toothpaste, comb, razor and soap; a small mirror; a spare set of socks; a photograph of Jocelyn Osgood leaning against the wing of a Spitfire; and a good bit of string which Gerald Perry Esquire had found on the floor of the Old Relics Society clubroom and had made Jim take because, as he often said, 'You never know when you'll need a good bit of string.'

Jim's sleeping blanket was rolled and wedged

between his back and the straps of his knapsack. Around his neck hung his binoculars and compass. He carried a small machete (which when not in use was always put into the scabbard on his belt), and his long black umbrella with the polished wooden handle (which made a good clearing implement and also kept him dry when necessary).

This was how the archaeologist–poet was equipped when he took his first step into that place below the mountain which always had a fine cloud rumbling quietly over it.

What struck Jim first about this strange new world were the colours of the jungle. His eyes had been accustomed to the browns and yellows of the Valley of the Kings, where the land was tree-less and the hills and valleys an unbroken slash of sand and dust. Here in the jungle though, there was very little yellow, and the only brown he could see was the rich, deep, dark brown of the soil and mulch on the forest floor. Everything else was green: dark green elephant-huge fronds bowing to the earth; olive-green vines winding around the grey-green branches of ancient trees; bright green shoots poking up through the moss-covered ground; and the gentle, even, green light filtering through the great, leafy canopy above.

Then there were the insects. Back home he was used to the mosquitoes and flies, which were generally small and harmless. It was very different here. There were mosquitoes, that was for certain, but of a size so vast and with a buzz so loud that Jim could hear them coming long before he saw them. When they zoomed close by his legs, they flew so fast their wings parted the hairs below his knees. And when he found himself walking by parts of the forest near river banks, where the mud and sand were exposed, he would be bombarded by legions of sand-flies, almost invisible to the sun-spectacled eye but with an itchy sting which soon let him know they had been and dined.

He found that his insect repellent was fairly useless: whenever he put it on it would dribble straight off again, caught in the beads of perspiration which flowed out of his pores like rivers. There was nothing for it but to swat.

There were other flying things, which Jim discovered early on his first day of trekking when he stopped to forage for morning tea. He was enjoying a banana when he noticed about twenty striped things buzzing at arm's length in front of him. They were all flying in what looked like the shape of a circle. When he reached out and poked his finger gently into the air where their flight path was, they immediately reformed and began to fly in the shape of an egg. 'How quaint,' he thought. He put another finger out, across from his first finger, and the group started to fly in the shape of a square. He then extended his pinkie finger beneath the last finger he had stuck out and twisted his hand slightly, and the flying formation became a rhombus. When he poked out his boot, they took on the pattern of a lopsided oblong. Upon sticking out his other boot (he was sitting down at the time), the shape became pointy at the bottom. Then he did a kind of squirmy dance and the shape went all wiggly but looked, as he had hoped, like the shape of Gerald Perry Esquire's head minus the ears.

He didn't do this for very long because he got a dreadful cramp in his toes, and anyway it appeared the stripy creatures had become tired of this game as they all flew off in the shape of the Madagascan coastline.

His first night brought a charming discovery. After he had washed himself in a small stream of running water and cleaned his teeth with water from his water bottle, he put out his fire and lay down on his sleeping blanket, staring up at the great fretwork of leaves far above him. He felt very small, almost a dot in this enormous place, but a happy and excited dot nonetheless, when from far up on high hundreds of tiny specks of light began to wink at him. He closed his eyes and opened them again to make sure he was not imagining it, but, no, there they were—brilliant yellow and green flicks of light, glowing one moment and gone the next. It was as though a city was suspended up there, with tiny lamps in tiny windows being turned on and off for his entertainment. He stared at them for some time until his exhaustion mingled with the symphony of jungle frog and cicada and sent him deeply to sleep.

On his third day away from civilisation, in the late afternoon, he clambered up a steep slope slippery with ferns. It was quite a climb and fairly skiddy, but by placing his boots carefully on the thick bracken instead of the muddy spots without greenery he was soon at the top.

He paused for breath and to wipe the steam from his sun-spectacles. Ahead he could see the dense jungle rising up towards a mountain—the dark mountain of HokeyCokey! Even with binoculars he could see no signs of any trails cut into the vegetation, nor any huts or villages, nor any tell-tale towers of smoke rising above the trees. There was no ChaCha Muchos visible at the pinnacle. Everything was quite untouched. HokeyCokey was swathed in cloud and waiting for him.

But to get there he had first to descend the other side of the steep slope he had just climbed. He lowered his binoculars and looked down. This side was equally as steep as the other and it looked even more muddy. There was less vegetation here. He took a deep breath, swatted at a particularly loud mosquito scudding towards his shin, and began to descend.

Now it was not uncommon for Cairo Jim to start making up poetry in his head whenever he was walking for long distances or feeling slightly unsure about where his next foot-hold ought to be. He found this helpful as it took his mind off the boredom or the uncertainty. Right now he was uncertain. It was a long way down to the bottom and he would rather arrive there on his two feet than on another part of his body not generally used for walking. So as he slowly put one foot ahead of the other, his poetry cells took over and he began speaking aloud:

'Here I am at end of world,
a place that is not boy-d or girl-d,
where monkeys howl and hornets hum,
where grows the wild——'

The next sound to come from his lips was not the word 'chrysanthemum'; it was a long, shocked,

'*Whoooooooaaaaahhhh*' as both his feet suddenly came level with his eyes and his backside became his rudder.

Down he went through mud and fern,
 down he went through bracken
  down he went through twig and palm
  —his sliding did not slacken!
   Muddy splashes on his hat,
    muddy trickles down his back,
     sliding this way, squelching that,
      down he went until he sat

IN A GREAT BIG PUDDLE THE COLOUR OF TEA.

He wriggled about in the cool murky water at the bottom of the slope, and a macaw whooped and laughed and squawked somewhere above.

'Well,' said Jim, wiping the smeary water from his sun-spectacles, 'that's one way of doing it.' He stood and waded out of the puddle, the water gushing from his shirt and shorts and boots.

He checked his equipment and was relieved to find everything as it should be, although of course the things not in his knapsack were now wet and brownish. He was not cut or scratched and only a little bruised.

He turned and took a step, and his boot slid in the mud. He got his balance again and took another step, but it was even muddier here, and suddenly he was battling to stay upright. His feet slid left and right and backwards and forwards, he bent at the waist to keep balanced, his hands flailed the air in crazy circles, trying to grab onto something to steady himself. Finally he thumped one boot down and it stayed firm, then he thumped down the other and it too found a solid spot. He stopped flailing and cautiously straightened his back.

With the smallest movement he unhooked his umbrella from his belt, intending to use it as a staff, and adjusted his pith helmet.

But right now the smallest movement was enough to topple the world from its axis, and the archaeologist–poet went sliding uncontrollably downwards, crashing through small ferns and ice-rink-slippery patches of lichens and fungi until, blinded by mud and leaf, he went crashing headfirst into a very deep, very dark hole.

*　　*　　*

'Whoah there,' rumbled Neptune Bone, pulling sharply on the camel's reins. The huge creature gave a loud snort and stopped in her tracks in the middle of the barren plain.

'Senor, why are we stopping here?' asked Dolores del Tempo, sitting on the camel's nether hump behind Bone.

'Good question,' croaked Desdemona, perched on his magenta-coloured fez.

'We are ages from the jungle,' Dolores protested.

'Down, you stupid beast,' ordered Bone. The camel snorted and obediently lowered herself, folding first her front legs, then her rear. The large man hoisted his leg over the hump and, in something of a sweaty jumble, slid to the ground. He swiped Desdemona from his fez and smoothed down his waistcoat impatiently.

'I know we are ages from the jungle, madam,' he smiled through clenched teeth. 'But there is some small business I need to perform here before we go on.' He pulled out his pocket-watch and squinted at it. 'Where is that slow little man? I can't think what's holding him up.'

Dolores looked up at the beating sun and dabbed at her neck with a small black lace handkerchief she had been dipping regularly into a big bottle of cologne. 'He'll be here, don't you worry, senor. He may not be good with things as a rule, but he is reliable.'

'Hrrmph,' snorted Bone. He took out a cigar, bit off the end, and spat it to the ground. 'About as reliable as a two-bob sundial if you ask me,' he muttered, pulling out his silver lighter.

On the road behind them there appeared a huge tumbling cloud of dust, accompanied by banging, groaning and scraping noises. The enormous raggle-taggle cloud was moving closer and closer, until finally it slowed down and stopped by the group.

'Ah, Senor von Mostetot,' came a voice from the dust. 'I thought I would never catch up. Phew, it is so hot...'

The gritty dust began to waft away, and a sweaty Mendoza stood before them, his broad chest heaving for air, his body bent almost double under the weight of Bone's travelling trunk, Dolores's three travelling trunks, her cosmetic cases and hat boxes, and a large colourful bundle of tent canvas. Tied to Mendoza's hips was the plough which he had been dragging along behind him.

He threw down his burdens and yanked his hair

into place. 'I would do anything for a drink of water,' he gasped.

'That can wait,' said Bone, scratching the dust from his beard. 'First, there's something important I need you to do.' He put his hand into his plus-fours pocket and withdrew a piece of faint yellow paper neatly folded in four. This he thrust at Mendoza. 'Have a good look,' he instructed bossily.

Mendoza unfolded the paper and examined it through his dusty eyelashes. He scrunched his face up tight, looked up at Bone, then looked back at the page. 'Senor?' he stammered.

'What's wrong?' asked Bone. 'Can't you read?'

Mendoza threw his head back and puffed out his chest. 'Of course I can read, senor! Who do you think you are talking to? Why, I'll have you know I am——' An abrupt change came over his face. 'I am happy to be at your service, senor.'

'Arrr,' arrred Bone, puffing on his cigar. 'Good fellow. Then this is what I want you to do: take that plough and attach it to this stupid beast——'

'Raaark!' squawked Desdemona. 'Who're you calling stupid?'

'Not that stupid beast, the *big* stupid beast——'

'That's better,' said Desdemona.

'——and take her out across the desert. Over there will do just fine. Then I want you to plough what you see written on that page into the ground. Do you understand?'

'All of this?'

'Yes,' said Bone, 'all of that. Don't leave anything

out. Copy it exactly. History depends on it. Do you understand?'

Mendoza nodded. 'Si.'

Bone blew a smoke ring into the dry air. 'But first you'll have to get Madam off,' he sneered.

At this point Dolores, who had been thinking about her complexion and not listening to the conversation, took some interest in the proceedings. 'What was that?' she asked.

'He said skedaddle,' squawked Desdemona.

Dolores shot her a filthy look. 'Senor von Mostetot,' she pouted furiously, 'kindly tell your crow-ny——'

'Har, har,' said the bird maliciously.

'——not to speak to me. It has fleas. And a most repugnant perfume.'

'*Craaaaaaaaaaarrrk!*'

'Back, Desdemona!' hissed Bone, grabbing the raven before she could strike. 'We still need her knowledge.'

The raven's feathers hackled and her claws arched. 'All right,' she throbbed. 'All right, all right, all right. But only for now. I'll get her. . .'

'Miss del Tempo.' Mendoza offered his hand. 'Oh, how beautiful you look today—such a sight for my itchy eyes—Miss del Tempo, I must ask you to step down for a little while. There is something I must do with this camello which, if you were to stay upon her hump, you would find very uncomfortable.'

'What do you mean?'

'Please come down. I will assist you. Here, take my hand, even though it is not worthy to touch the heel of your stiletto.'

Dolores looked down at him. 'All right,' she frowned. 'It's about time I stood on terra firma again. A girl could get seasick up here.' She gave Mendoza her hand and he guided her to the ground.

'Right,' said Bone. He went to the camel's saddlebags and found his megaphone. 'I'll direct you through this. Tie the plough to the beast, and work her at a pace, otherwise the blades won't dig deep enough into the dirt. I want this deed to last for all Eternity!'

'Si, senor,' sighed Mendoza. He untied the plough from himself and dragged it over to the camel. As he fastened it to her he whispered soothingly into her ear. 'Ah, don't you worry, you cousin of our llama. You are big and strong like Mendoza, si? Si. Come, we shall be amigos on this journey. What do you say?'

The big, strong Bactrian snorted and shook her head in a circular motion (which is camelspeak for 'You bet your poncho we will').

'Make it snappy!' Bone bellowed through the megaphone, puffing a chimney-stack of smoke at the same time.

'Si, senor,' sighed Mendoza, winking at the camel. He ran to the end of the plough and turned it and the beast towards the plain.

Perched on a dusty rock, Desdemona pecked a flea from her belly and, through slitted eyes, watched intently as the short man and the huge camel began to carry out Bone's naughty deed.

*   *   *

Dusk was hovering over the deep hole like a panther waiting to pounce.

It had been a grim afternoon for the archaeologist–poet. For the first hour after he had fallen into the pit he had tried to climb the sheer muddy walls, but it had been hopeless—no matter where he climbed he soon slid straight back to the bottom. He had lit matches to try and illuminate any twigs or roots which may have been jutting out through the mud, things that would have made firm handles or footholds, but there had been nothing within reach. He had paced back and forth, his hands clasped resolutely behind his back as he had tried to think of a way to escape. But no lightning bolts of cleverness had zinged in on him and now, as the twilight became more panther-like by the minute, he began to fear he would be stuck down here for all time. Maybe one day somebody would find his pith helmet half-buried in the mud, and the world would know what had happened to Cairo Jim. Oh, if only he had some poetry published before now...

He sat on his rolled and muddied sleeping blanket and looked up. Already the dark-earthed rim at the top of the hole was beginning to blur against the dimness above it.

The best thing to do now, he thought, would be to light a fire to protect himself from any savage intruder who might decide to pay him a visit during the night. High above, the jungle was turning up its night music. First there was a single croak which startled Jim with its sudden loudness. Then another croak sounded, as if answering the first one, and then the first one answered back more loudly, then another came from somewhere further away, and soon the whole place was belching and cracking fit to burst the sky. He shuddered and peered through the thickening dark for any dry wood.

Then something happened which made him freeze.

As the last rays of light began to dissolve, another sound came, a sound which startled and chilled him. A sound on the surface of the ground high above. A sort of squelchy dragging. Then it stopped.

Jim listened as closely as he could for it to happen again. Seconds passed, seconds that seemed like centuries. His heart beat like a tom-tom.

Then the noise came back.

What was it? He shut his eyes and concentrated. It was a rustling, he decided. No, it was more like a dragging. No, it rustled again, squelching at the same time. Now it was dragging, getting louder. Squelch, drag. Squelch, drag. Rustle, squelch, drag. And then it stopped.

Small beads of moisture broke out on Cairo Jim's forehead. The noise was coming closer, approaching the hole. *Whatever was up there knew he was below!*

His mind wheeled and rattled as he tried to work out what to do. Something up there was after him, and it had him right where it wanted him to be— trapped, helpless, in a hole. He had to do something to protect himself. But what? What could he do, all the way down here?

He would call out, he thought. He would put on a scary voice and try to frighten this thing away. He would shout 'Rack off' like Esmond Horneplush, a grouchy man from the Old Relics Society who used such language whenever someone sat in his personal armchair. Yes, that was what he would do. He opened his mouth and thought 'Esmond Horneplush' and was about to shout out in his best blustery manner when something struck him sharply on the pith helmet.

Klunk!

Cairo Jim reeled and sprang up. Above him there was a small dragging noise and then what sounded like a mighty disturbance of air as something beat through it. And then there was only the croaking of the jungle again.

Jim fumbled in his pockets for his matches. With trembling hands he lit one and shone the light around the walls of his prison. His eyes almost bulged out of his head.

There where he had been sitting was a long, plaited vine stretching from the bottom of the hole all the way up to the surface of the earth.

'Well, sharpen my head and call me a pyramid,' whispered Cairo Jim.

He stared at it for a long time, moving his match up and down until the flame burnt his fingers. Then he reached out and gave it a good tug. It didn't budge. Whoever or whatever had thrown it to him had fastened it securely above.

Jim listened carefully for any sign of his vine-thrower, but all he heard was the deep music of the forest night. If the vine-thrower was up there, he thought, it surely would have made some kind of noise by now. It might even peer down to see why he hadn't come up. But he hadn't seen any eyes glowing in the darkness, and he hadn't heard any sudden noises close to the rim of the hole. And so, after half an hour of listening, he made a decision. His heart beating wildly, he gathered all his things, secured them around his body, and started to heave himself up the vine, trying to be mousequiet all the way.

It seemed like ages, that climb to the top. He swivelled back and forth, his hands slick with moisture and his knees knocking together annoyingly. He dared not think of what might be waiting above, but he decided that as soon as he set foot on solid ground again, he would pelt off into the undergrowth and find a good tree to climb. Nothing was going to get him.

At last he was within a hand's length of the forest floor. He took a deep breath, placed first one hand and then the other on the ground above his head, and swung his legs up over the muddy edge and hoisted himself out of the hole. Then he jumped up, held onto his pith helmet, and took off into the charcoal shadows, like a creature possessed.

6

MORE STRIFE FOR CAIRO JIM

THE next morning Jim woke on a branch of a gigantic calabash tree where he had spent an uncomfortable and nervous night.

He stretched and scratched himself and looked up at the cover of leaves above. The early beams of sunlight were piercing through the green, and all about him birds, monkeys and loud insects were waking up for the new day. He gathered his knapsack and equipment from the broad cradle of the branch and began to climb down, being careful not to bang his head on the huge pieces of gourd-like fruit hanging everywhere above and beneath him.

Setting his boots on the muddy forest floor, he looked around warily for any sign of his vine-thrower. But as far as he could see there was nothing. He did not know how far he was from the hole. All he could remember after he had escaped was running as fast as he could, skidding through small plants and crashing through dark twigs and sharp needly branches until he had run headfirst into the trunk of the calabash tree. Because this was sturdier than his head (his head had pounded whereas the tree hadn't even trembled) he decided it would be a good place to hide.

'Hmm,' he said aloud. He took his compass and opened the cover. 'North, I think.' And, stepping carefully on the sludgy floor, that was the direction he took.

After almost three hours of sloshy terrain, during which he had to push through dense glistening fronds and crowded thick branches, he stumbled upon a thin strip of dirt winding up a small hilly slope. On either side of this trail the vegetation grew as though the leaves and boughs had some time ago been cleared back.

Cairo Jim's heart fluttered. He unstrapped his knapsack and let it drop to the ground. 'Now,' he said very loudly to the greenness, 'we are getting somewhere!' He looked through his binoculars towards the top of the trail, to a place where it widened into a small, dry clearing. He took a drink of water from his water bottle, put his knapsack on again, and, with a spring in his mud-caked boots, was on his way.

It took Jim longer to get to the clearing than he had expected. In the jungle, trails can be very deceptive. Distances appear very different. Jim discovered this when, after nearly an hour of climbing, he stood in the middle of the clearing, puffing and panting, and looked back to the point from where he had started. It appeared to be only a hop, skip and jump away.

He picked his shirt from his chest, shaking it up and down to try and cool himself a little. He took off his knapsack and wiped the sweat from his brow and chin and from under his pith helmet. The higher he had climbed, the hotter it had got. The air was now quite steamy.

The clearing in which Jim stood was bordered by

old, gnarled orange trees. 'Champion,' thought Jim, 'morning tea.' The trees were overgrown and had not been tended in a long time and were probably, he thought, once part of a tribe's plantation. This part of the cloudforest had once been inhabited.

But when he picked some of the delicious-looking oranges he found them riddled with fruitfly and small, slimy grubs with wicked, crimson eyes. He threw the fruit into the jungle and took out a tin of preserved peaches. At least he had those, he thought a little sadly.

As he tucked in to his peaches, far above him, far above the canopy of leaves which still blocked out the sky, the clouds were gathering like giant grey pillowcases billowing in the wind.

At four o'clock that afternoon the trail ended sharply and Cairo Jim stepped out from under the great leafy canopy. He was standing on the slope of a river bank, and for the first time since he had entered the cloudforest he could see sky again.

Hanging low overhead was a monstrous, enormous, heavy-as-a-million-years sheet of dark, dark grey. Large blobs of rain began to fall, thudding onto his pith helmet and splattering down his shirt. The rain made the air cooler and brought a light, delicate mist which danced along in sweeping patches here and there on the rushing surface of the river.

Jim removed his sun-spectacles and looked into the distance. His lips started to curl into a smile and his eyes narrowed and widened. Beyond the river, and enveloped in mist and clouds, was a huge black hulking shape rising steeply towards the sheet of dark grey sky.

'HokeyCokey,' he sang quietly, over and over. 'HokeyCokey, HokeyCokey, HokeyCokey. Here I come!'

He put his sun-spectacles into his pocket, adjusted his knapsack, and proceeded to find a safe way of getting down the slippery river-bank. If he made a mistake he could go crashing down into the water which he could hear gurgling below the lush, rain-soaked carpet of ferns and palms. He braced himself, found his balance, and down he went.

His judgment had been good and soon he was standing on level ground at the river's edge. He took out his map and unfolded it carefully, trying not to get it too soggy. 'Now let's see...,' he pondered as he ran his index finger gently along the jungle he had come through. There was a long narrow strip of blue, and with his fingernail he scored an invisible line beneath the name of this strip: MARJANGOWER RIVER. To the left of his finger, about three kilometres along according to the map's scaled distance, there was another name: MARJANGOWER FALLS, and to the right, not far from where he was now standing, a series of small dots in the centre of the strip of blue represented the MARJANGOWER RAPIDS. Underneath this name, in small italics, was printed a single word: *treacherous*.

Jim looked down at the swift current. It seemed as though some huge being somewhere further down river had pulled up a plug in the riverbed, and every drop of water was rushing towards the unseen plug-hole. The turbulence must be from the Rapids, he thought. He put his map away again and looked across the river. The stretch of water was not very wide, only about five metres from here to the other side. The problem was how to cross it.

Even if the water in the middle of the river was only waist deep, the current looked strong enough to easily knock him over and sweep him down to the Falls, so wading across was definitely out. Maybe, he thought, he could build a simple boat. He could chop down a tree, light a fire and smoke the trunk, then strip away the outer casing of strong bark and mould it over suitably shaped rocks, covering it with gooey tree sap as he went, until it was watertight. He shook his head slowly; *that* would take him nearly a month at the least. There must be some other way.

He turned his gaze upriver and there, through the sleeting rain, he saw it: a slender tree, growing at the water-line, had had its roots dislodged by the current and had fallen straight across the water, its uppermost branches resting on the opposite bank. 'Ah-ha,' he muttered. He put up his umbrella and scampered towards this makeshift bridge.

Standing next to it, he prodded it with his boot. It did not move. Even though it looked slender, it was obviously heavy enough not to have been carried off by the flow. He got down on all fours and, placing his head close to the branches, checked the line of the trunk. It was almost straight and quite smooth, and in the middle bowed only slightly towards the river. Quite negotiable, he decided. But first, in way of preparation, he would have to follow the procedures he had learnt at archaeology school in his Jungle Expedition classes.

He left his knapsack and sleeping blanket by the

river and ventured a small way into the jungle with only his machete. There he cut down two thin but very strong poles of bamboo, each of them about four metres in length, and took them back to the fallen tree. These would be his 'balancers' and without them the crossing would prove too risky.

He put the machete into its scabbard, and put the scabbard into the knapsack. Then, with a mighty effort, he hurled the knapsack towards the other side of the river.

Through the air it twirled and twirled, its shoulder straps flapping like drenched brown wings. It was heading straight for an overhanging branch of a vine-choked tree, and suddenly, as it came close, one of the straps caught on an offshoot from this branch. With a violent jerk the knapsack stopped twirling several metres above the bank, as though time had stopped and suspended it in limbo.

Cairo Jim smiled. He picked up his umbrella and threw it like a javelin to the opposite side. It speared through the raindrops and with a *sklerrch* the silver pointy end sank into the muddy bank.

The archaeologist–poet pulled down the chinstrap from the brim of his pith helmet, fastened it under his chin, and picked up the bamboo poles.

At this moment, two things happened: the rain became much heavier, as though a great reservoir in the heavens had cracked and broken, sending its load bucketing down all at once onto this very spot, and (the second thing) a thought struck Cairo Jim. He realised that even though he had learned the technique of how to cross a raging river using only two bamboo poles and a fallen tree trunk when he was at archaeology school, he had never actually *done* it.

This thought made him frown. Then his knees started, with the slightest of movement, to knock together. Then the back of his neck became itchy, and his armpits began to drip and his stomach felt like it had knots of silk tied in it. Before he knew it, he was a bundle of nervousness.

He stood there, very still (except for his knees which were fast becoming almost inseparable), clutching the two poles tightly on either side of him. He stared fixedly at the rage of water. The raindrops were now striking the surface like bullets, heavy bullets which shot small fountainsquirts of river into the air. The current was flowing over the middle of the tree trunk, staining the wood a dark, murky colour, and it was flowing so loudly it was hard for Jim to think properly. He watched the level carefully. Elsewhere, away from the middle, the water was about a metre beneath the trunk, and rising. Jim knew he must move soon. Still his knees knocked.

All of a sudden a huge flock of macaws came swooping between him and the opposite bank, with a cry so ear-shattering it jolted him out of his nervousness. *Raaaaaaaarrrrrk!* They flew in a wide circle before they disappeared above the treetops.

'Come on, Jim,' he said quietly to himself. 'Pull yourself together. It's only a *little* river, after all. Just a few quick steps and then you're on your way again. This rain will let up soon. Remember the Society motto: "Old Relics Get Older By The Minute, And So Do You".'

He took a huge breath and, with trepidation pumping through his veins, planted both feet firmly on the trunk. 'Think of this, Jim,' he told himself, 'think of the look of flabbergastedness on Miss Osgood's face when she hears the news that you've found the City. Think of the pleasure you'll have when you tell her of it in person.' He mustered all these thoughts together, holding them tightly in his brain.

Then he lifted the left bamboo pole with his left hand and plunged it forward into the torrent. It sank a little way into the soft mud of the riverbed and he could see the water level here was about a metre deep. He did the same with the right pole. When both poles were firmly standing (but not too firmly, otherwise he wouldn't be able to pull them up again), he took his first, slidy step along the trunk. That was easy. Now he was standing between both poles. He lifted the left pole again and moved it forward. The rain was pelting down so hard now he had to keep his eyes half-shut in order to see. Up came the right pole and forward it went. The river here was about a metre-and-a-half deep.

Now the next step. Slowly he took it, first the left foot sliding uncertainly along, then the right. This foot slid completely off the trunk and Jim had to lean heavily against the right pole to regain his balance. The pole, being strong, took his weight, and once again he was standing between both poles, his heart palpitating wildly.

The next step he was to take would put him at that place on the trunk where the water was gushing over it, directly in the middle of the river. He took a breath, steadied himself, and moved the pole on his left back and forth to loosen the bottom of it from the muddy bed. Then he lifted it and moved it forward.

Squeelchh. It sank nearly three metres, and Jim had to half squat to keep holding onto it. He gulped; he hadn't reckoned it would be so deep. The water was rushing up over the tops of his boots and he could feel his socks getting cooler in the toe regions.

He reached behind, still holding onto the now almost vanished left pole, and grabbed the other one with his right hand. Levering it back and forth, he extracted it from the mud and was moving it forward, pushing it against the fierce current, when in an instant a huge surge of water smacked against both him and the pole and sent the bamboo flying off downriver as though it were a torpedo!

Jim grabbed onto the left pole with both hands, just in time, for at that moment the water swept his feet completely off the trunk. He wrapped his legs around the pole, but the water was rising fast, swirlingly rising, past his knees, past his thighs, up his back, until the tremendous force of it snapped the pole in two.

Cairo Jim swivelled and fell backwards into the mainflow, his pith helmet coming loose and floating swiftly away. He went under the water, resurfaced and, through a blinding flash of bubbles, saw his hat bobbing and diving as it coursed downstream. Desperate, he clutched into the air for anything he could hold, but there was nothing; he was being swept past boulders worn too smooth to grab. The water pounded his ears, his temples, his kneecaps. Under he went again, dragged gurglingly down. Then a huge rip forced him upwards.

His face got nearer and nearer to the surface; he looked up through the sheet of water between him and air, and through the bubbles and mud he saw a great rush of blue and gold right above him.

There was a mighty scream, loud enough to wake the dead, and that was the last thing Cairo Jim heard.

7

A Curious Camp

Mendoza had not had time to scratch himself. The Bone–von Mostetot–del Tempo expedition was now in the cloudforest and the tireless porter had spent all the afternoon clearing a large circle of jungle and then erecting Bone's ornate tent-pavilion and Dolores's smaller but still flashy tentette. After this he had walked for seven kilometres until he found fresh water, and then carted it back to the campsite.

He poured some of the water into a large dish and took it to the massive camel who sat chewing in a corner of the clearing. 'Here you are, my amiga,' he puffed, setting the dish in front of her. He ruffed up the patch of twisty hair that sprouted between her ears, and crouched before her. 'Ah, I am so glad Senor von Mostetot allowed you to stay with us after the ploughing was done. But I had to plead with him, si?'

The silent beast blinked her long-lashed eyes and rolled her head in a circle.

'Do you know, I think he was planning to leave you out in the desert all by yourself. He is a strange man, that one. The way he and the bird smell. Prunes, I think. And those clothes he wears. They are so...so...' He frowned.

'Quaaooo?' she snorted.

'Exactly!' Mendoza said happily. 'The very word I was looking for.' He curled his upper lip, bared his teeth, and snorted loudly. The camel smiled and brought her head close to his neck. He snorted again, even more loudly, then giggled in a snortish sort of way.

'Mendoza!' came an impatient shout.

'Ah,' he whispered, 'it is Miss del Tempo. She wants her water and I have been dilly-dallying. Now I am in for it.' He stood, stretched his legs, and bent close to her ear. 'But have no worries, her bark is much worser than her bite. I should know. Adios for now.'

'Quaao.'

'Hold onto your alpacas, senorita,' he called, 'I have it here. Fresh and cold just for you.'

'Well don't hang about like a stunned tarantula. Bring it in!'

'Si, Miss del Tempo.' He lifted the door-flap and lurched in with the bucket, spilling a great deal on the ground.

'And be careful! You'll leave me with nothing to remove my daytime makeup.'

'Sorry, senorita.'

'You have never been good with water as a rule.'

Dolores del Tempo was sitting before a hefty wooden makeup case, which was resting on one of her smaller travelling trunks. This case had two doors at the side, both with mirrors on them, and a hinged, mirrored flap at the top. All three mirrored surfaces were opened wide and in the centre were three long shelves packed chock full of lipsticks, eyebrow pencils, rouges, false eyelashes, powders, puffs and sponges. Mendoza poured some water into a bowl between Dolores and the mirrors.

'Gracias, senor,' Dolores said. She ran her fingers through her slicked back hair, and pulled a face as though half of her was about to cry and the other half was about to explode.

'What is the matter, Miss del Tempo?'

'Look at my hair, Mendoza. It is *feelthy*.'

'Ah, but you still look divine, senorita.' He sat on the ground behind her and admired her in the mirrors.

'And my face. . .look, the dust is everywhere, like icing on a cake.'

'Some water will help you,' he said, quietly and calmly. She glanced at him in the mirror and then a very small smile lifted the corners of her lips. 'You are right, Mendoza.' Taking a big sea sponge, she dipped it into the bowl and started to wipe her face.

'Forgive me for being so inquisitive, senorita, but there is something I do not understand. . .'

'What?' said Dolores.

'Well, with all these dusty roads and the burning sun and now with the jungle and the hardships and the bities it will bring, why did you wish so desperately to come along on this expedition? What is so important about ChaCha Muchos for you?'

She stopped sponging and gave him a long look. Then she laid down the sponge and turned to face him. 'Look,' she said, pointing to that part of her face where her cheek joined the side of her nostril. 'Do you see? That is the reason!'

Mendoza looked closely. 'But I see nothing, senorita.'

'You are being kind, Mendoza. You are trying to save me from this fate worse than death itself. But don't bother. *I* can see it.' She gave a huge pout of a frown.

'See what?'

'*My wrinkle!*' She ran her finger up and down her cheek, as if trying to smudge the thing away before it spread. 'Si, my amigo, I am getting older. Soon there will be many more. It starts with just one you know, a tiny thing like the finest cobweb, but soon another one appears and then another and another, and before you know what's hit you, your face looks like the backside of an elephant.' She turned and started sponging again. 'Then how will I *ever* find my aristocrat?' she whimpered to the mirrors.

'One day your Prince will come,' Mendoza said. He smiled at her reflection. 'Ah, Miss del Tempo, beauty comes from the inside.'

'Hrrmph,' she sniffed.

'But I still do not understand. What has a tiny wrinkle——'

'Oh!'

'——got to do with ChaCha Muchos?'

She spun around. 'Because, Mendoza, ChaCha Muchos holds the key to the getting rid of it!'

The wonky-haired man looked more puzzled than ever.

'I will tell you something,' she whispered. 'Something you must promise not to tell another living soul . . .'

'I promise,' he said.

'There is a legend that the City of ChaCha Muchos was built not by the Dancers from Cuzco, but by an isolated tribe of Indians who used a potion to evaporate the rocks on top of HokeyCokey Mountain.'

Mendoza gasped.

'Nobody knows what was in this potion, but the story goes that it could destroy everything except leather. Think of *that*, Mendoza! Think of what you could do if you were able to get your hands on a potion such as that!'

'Oh, Miss del Tempo...'

She straightened her back and looked down at him from her great height. 'I have come along on this expedition because I am hoping to find the descendants of those Indians. The City itself is not important to me. What matters is that *potion*.'

'And if they still have it, and you get it? What then?'

'Then I shall take it back to Lima and find a way to dilute it. It would be far too strong to apply in its pure state. If it could burn straight through hard rocks, imagine what it could do to the human skin!'

'You mean——?'

'Yes, Mendoza! I will produce the greatest wrinkle remover ever known to humankind! It will even be better than used teabags or sliced cucumbers or yoghurt facepacks! I will set up a huge factory and mass-produce it in little pink glass bottles with an adhesive picture of myself on the front. I shall call it ''Peruvian Dolores's Really Revolutionary Wrinkle Remover'', if I can fit it all on the label, and I will sell a million bottles!'

'Oh my goodness, gracious me,' said Mendoza.

'And then, once again, I shall be beautiful,' she sighed. 'And richer.'

Mendoza thrummed his fingers on his kneecap. 'Do you think Senor von Mostetot knows of this potion?'

'Him? Ha! I am sure he has no idea. He is only interested in finding his precious setting for this motion picture he wants to produce. His beloved ''epic''. Don't worry, Mendoza, I know these movie people. They do not exist outside their own little world.'

'Si, Miss del Tempo,' said Mendoza, swatting at a mosquito.

Over in the tent-pavilion, another plan was about to be revealed.

A dirgey Wurlitzer tune was pumping out of the gramophone as Neptune Bone lay sprawled on his inflatable chaise-longue (which Mendoza had almost burst his lungs inflating), doing a fine manicure on his pudgy hands. Desdemona perched on top of his travelling trunk, itself the size of a small automobile. Her beak was deep in a tin of spinach-green seaweed, and she was slurping disgustingly.

'Arrr. If you can't ingest that more quietly,' the large man rumbled, 'then go outside.'

She looked up at him, her one open eye throbbing the colour of blood. She whipped out her yellow tongue and caught a piece of the green goo stuck to the top of her skull. 'Craaark!' she replied, but 'Bloated brute,' she thought.

'And don't look at me in that manner.' He swiped at a zapping insect. 'Blast this jungle! Not only do

I have to put up with Madam and Wonky-hair out there, and you in here, but I've also got to contend with a zillion micro nuisances as well. Arrrrr!' He pulled out a cigar and lit it, blowing the smoke at the nearest mosquito.

'My Captain,' the raven croaked, 'there's something we have yet to discuss.'

'What?' snapped the fez-wearing man, squirming on the chaise-longue.

'The matter of payment.'

'Payment?' His eyes widened. 'Payment?' He sniffed four times, like a steam locomotive starting up. '*Payment?*' His cheeks became bright and his eyebrows bristled.

'Yep, payment.'

Bone clenched the cigar in his teeth and buffed his fingernails with agitated strokes. 'Oh well,' he mumbled, 'that's easy. I'll just give Madam some of those cheap plastic baubles. That should make her eyes light up.'

'The only way to do that'd be to shine a torch in her ears,' said Desdemona. 'No, Captain, I don't mean payment for *her*, I mean payment for *me*.'

'What? For you? Don't be insane.'

The raven picked up the empty seaweed tin with her strong claw and hurled it across the tent. It crashed against one of the tent poles and clattered to the floor. 'Insane? Insane? Nevermore!'

'You should count yourself lucky I've allowed you to accompany me at all. Remember, bird, I could have easily dobbed you in to the Antiquity Squad.'

She pecked a munching flea from her tarsus and

gave him the most dastardly glare. 'Three can play at that game,' she snarled (she was never good at adding). 'You're not the only one who can blackmail. If you don't pay me for this trip and for all the work I'm doing on it, I'll tell the Antiquity Squad about your plans to melt down the doors of the Cairo Museum. I'll tell them the whole story!'

'Ha! They'd throw a hessian bag over your head and rush you straight to the ravengallows.'

'They'd have to catch me first. I'm not as stupid as you think. I wouldn't tell them bird to person, oh, no, I'd put a hanky over my beak and ring them on the telephone. They'd never get me. Hahahahahahaha!'

'You couldn't dial it with those feathers,' he smirked.

'I'd do it with a pencil.'

Bone became very still and watched her through slitted eyes. The cigar smoke lingered like a heavy cloud above him. He had little choice. She had him in the palm of her claw. If he did not go along with her she would blurt out the whole thing, and his best-laid plan, his plan of Utter Genius, would be undone like runny cheese left out in the sun.

'Arrr,' he growled. 'All right, you treacherous toady, I'll pay you something. After we've grabbed all that glittering gold, I'll give you a small piece as a token of my esteem. Perhaps a coin or something.'

Desdemona hopped up onto the edge of the gramophone and kicked the needle savagely across the record. There was a noise like shattering glass.

'How dare you?' rumbled Bone, astounded by this deed.

'It's not gold I want,' she croaked. 'Gold is no use to me. I have no pockets in which to put it. No, what I want is something that'll *adorn* me. Something that'll break up all this blecchness.' She ran her wings over her body in a frantic gesture, like someone playing the harp.

'Like what?' sneered Bone, beginning to get curious.

'Like a necklace.'

'A necklace, eh? Arrr.' He took a long puff and let the air fume through his nostrils. 'Well, greedy guts, there are plenty of necklaces in the Museum.'

'Craaark! But not the sort of necklace I desire.'

'They have many kinds there.'

'But not made from the toes of a human being, have they?'

'*What?*' Even Neptune Bone was shocked.

'As my payment I want a necklace made of eight toes from the foot of a human being.'

'By Jove,' he gasped.

'But not *any* human being,' she continued. 'Oh, no siree, this human being must be very, very tall, a bad violinist, an expert on Peruvian history, and of the female variety. And she must sing at a club known as the Popocatepetl Club.'

'What kind of evil is this?' Bone asked, almost in awe.

'The best kind. *My* evil.' She was now hopping up and down excitedly. 'I want to peck four toes from each of Dolores del Tempo's feet, then I shall string them together on a gold chain which you will give me from your fob-watch, and I will have a necklace the likes of which no other raven has ever worn. And others will take notice of me. I can even change my appearance by painting the toenails a different colour every now and then.'

'But Desdemona, she won't be able to stand up. She'll fall flat on her face.'

'What a pity. *Craaaaaaark!*' She opened her wings and did five quick cartwheels across the ground.

'What a fearsome flying felon you are.' Bone's eyes glinted through the smoke. 'All right!' He clapped his hands loudly. 'So be it. Seeing as how I'm such a generous chap as what I am, you shall *have* your necklace. But only after Madam has shown us where our City is.'

'Craaark. I knew you'd see things my way,' gloated Desdemona, her tongue hanging out and dribbling.

'Arrr, now come and lick my spats clean. They're filthy.'

Outside, the camel was half-dozing in the fading light, watching the hundreds of magical fireflies playing high above against the ceiling of leaves.

She was not an ordinary camel. In fact, before she had been captured and sold to Neptune Bone at Honest Ahmed's Used Camel Yard, she had come from the Wonder Herd of Thebes. She was wise and calm, and did not mind being in the cloudforest, or resent being mistreated by Bone and the raven, or even ache for being so far from home.

She knew there was a reason for it all, and she knew she only had to wait for it to show itself. After all, as no less a person than Neptune Bone often said, 'Time will reveal all'.

8

A MOST IMPORTANT MEETING

THE pith helmet of Cairo Jim sat upside down in a clearing below the foothills of HokeyCokey Mountain, its white cotton covering spattered and stained a washed-out, murky brown.

Nearby, his knapsack and sleeping blanket, still hanging from the branch, swung backwards and forwards in the falling wind. His umbrella still stuck out from the muddy bank.

The rain had almost stopped and the jungle had become very quiet.

The archaeologist–poet was lying face down on a grassy patch above the river. He was not awake, but not fully asleep; he was somewhere in that slumbery underworld where one often finds oneself after a huge disruptive experience. Through his closed eyelids he could sense the light and the shadows dancing around him. His drenched and pounding ears could hear the whispers of the wind as it rose and fell, buffeting gently against the branches overhead. Somewhere downwind he could hear the river, its gurgle much less fierce than when it had swallowed him up. He gave a small groan and rolled over onto his back. The leaves above him stirred, rustling and hissing as the breeze threaded through them, and in his gurgled, clammy state he heard their taunts: 'A fool...a fool...I met a fool in the forest.'

His senses gradually started coming back to him, and the taunts started getting louder: 'A fool...a motley fool...a miserable fool.'

Then they became very high-pitched and screechy: 'As I do live by food, I met a fool.'

Suddenly something was hopping up and down on his chest! He opened his eyes wide and jerked his head forward. Straight away his nose rammed into a smooth, curved beak of alabaster whiteness. Above it, two beady, dark, blinking eyes stared back at his own, full of curiosity.

Cairo Jim recoiled, and the most beautiful gold-and-blue-feathered macaw he had ever seen sprang from him and fluttered over to his pith helmet. She perched on its brim and lowered her head, still keeping her eyes fixed firmly on him.

'So,' she screeched loudly, her voice making his eyebrows stand on end. 'Welcome to the brave new world.'

Jim sat up, his mouth open. 'You...you can talk?'

'Of course I can talk,' the bird said. She opened up her huge wings—the span was well over a metre—and closed them again. 'You can fly?' she asked.

'Er, no. Not by myself, at least.'

'Raaark! Methinks you couldn't. Otherwise you would have shot out of that water like a toucan late for tea.'

'You saw me down there?'

'Of course I saw you down there. How else would

I have saved you from your outcast state if I hadn't seen you?'

'I don't understand,' Jim frowned, scratching the back of his neck. 'You...you *rescued* me?'

'I did indeed,' she squawked, raising her wings and lowering them again. 'I wrapped the Grip-vine around your leg and winched you out.'

'Why, thank you. Thank you very much.' He squeezed the water out of his hair, and frowned again. 'You rescued me by *yourself*?'

'By myself I rescued you. Of course. The other macaws won't have anything to do with beings of the human species. They don't trust them.'

'Really?'

'Raark.'

'Do you?' asked Jim.

'Not as a rule. But you seem not like the others. You appear to be of a more thoughtful step. And you do not hack our jungle away as though it is a new thing that will keep on springing forth quickly. No, I've beheld you. When you bend back the ferns and leaves, it is almost as though you do not want to. Methinks you know that all of this is as ancient as the hills. Raark. Methinks you have a great degree of respect for things older than yourself.'

She hopped off the hat and waddled around the grass, circling him and watching his eyes with her own. She blinked often and this suggested to Jim that she was of a considerable age, as macaws are inclined to be. There was also something in the way she hopped every now and then which gave him the feeling that she didn't *entirely* trust him.

'You've been watching me then?' he asked.

'Raark! Ever since you and that other human being with hair the colour of ochre-mud almost flew into us in the noisy metallic bird, I have been watching you. It nearly blew our feathers away, that smelly, noisy thing.'

'I'm sorry,' said Jim. 'We didn't see you until the last minute.'

She quickly lowered her head to the grass and pecked up a small football-shaped nut which she cracked loudly in her beak. 'I accept your apology,' she prowked as she swallowed the insides of it. 'And I will tell you something: you have given me quite a lot of mirth.'

'Oh, yes?' said Jim.

'Reerk,' she nodded. 'When you went sliding like a wild Peruvian boar all the way down that hill into the pit, I laughed so much my beak flipped up into my face. It was devilishly hard to get it down again.'

'You saw me fall in?'

'Who else d'you think tossed down the vine?'

'Well I'll be swoggled,' gasped Cairo Jim.

The bird kept circling. 'Swoggled? Swoggled? I do not understand your meaning.'

'Well,' he said, 'it means. . .it means. . .oh, never mind. Tell me something, will you please?'

'Quiet!' she screeched, her eyes now all at once big and glaring. 'Do not move! Hold thy breath!'

What happened next happened so quickly, so instantaneously, that if Jim had not been there he would never have believed it. The great bird shot up into the leaves like a spear of quicksilver light and then down she came even faster, swooping close to the ground and coming to perch on a branch not far from his shoulder. She tossed her head around and snapped her beak open and shut eight times, very rapidly.

Then she fluttered down and perched gracefully on the toe of his boot. She spat a hairy mouthful onto his knee.

'It was coming straight for you,' she prerked.

Jim looked hard at the chewed-up mess. 'What is. . .what *was* it?'

'A HokeyCokey Dancing Tarantula. Oh, what a tangoed web they weave. If it'd got you, you'd have been as stiff as a cayman's snout by morning.'

'Goodness,' gulped Jim. He brushed the mess away.

'It is obvious,' the bird declared, peering up at the skies, 'that you need some looking after. I have never seen a single human thing land in so many pickles.' She sighed. 'Beings of the human species do not belong here, it is a well-known fact around these parts.'

'Have there been many of us here?'

'Occasionally you come through the jungle, sometimes in flocks, sometimes alone. And there was the man in white, with trousers like yours, but longer—right down to the bumps on the side of his feet—and a torso-covering the same colour with little circular pearl-shell things that went through holes, and hidden nests from which he produced things to wipe his nose. *He* stayed with me for a long time. Until the noisy metallic bird came and took him. . .'

She hopped off his boot and waddled around in small, distracted circles, her browfeathers ruffling.

'Was he your friend?' Jim asked.

'I thought so,' she prowked. 'He seemed to like me. He taught me more words. And he left me the book.'

'The book?'

She nodded and licked her beak. 'Raark, what a marvel it is! It has delighted me more than anything I can recall. It has carried me along on imaginary winds to lands I would never have known.' Her beak began to crease at the edges, and Jim realised this was the nearest thing a bird gets to a smile.

'Let me tell you something,' she crooned, her voice becoming warbly. 'Before I began reading the book methought that all beings of the human species were wilder than my animal colleagues. All I ever saw when the upright-walkers came here were their blunderbuss ways and their savage scimitars. These creatures left trails of havoc and destruction behind them, blazing like fires. But when I read the book I came to realise that not *all* of your sort were like that. Oh, no. Why, I thought that if a *single human being* could write all those beautiful words and all those wonderful jokes and could tell all those exciting stories—some that made me weep, some that made me laugh, some that made me very scared—and all those lyrical poems, then there must be hope for you two-legs after all!'

Jim leaned forward and clasped his knees. 'What is this book?' he asked, stirred by her passion. 'What is it called?'

She stopped waddling and looked at his eyes. 'It is very well-known amongst you humans. You have probably read it, I daresay. . .what a specimen of your race that writer was. . .'

'Who wrote it? What is it called?'

'Raaark! Too many questions for today! I shall tell you tomorrow.' She hopped across to his hat and nudged it with her beak. 'A very jaunty pith helmet you have,' she chirped.

Jim looked at it somewhat sadly. 'It used to be much cleaner,' he sighed. 'So much whiter.'

She turned to him. 'So tell me,' she said briskly. 'You didn't come here into this dark and different place to get your hat dirty or to slide down mudbanks or to fall into holes or to nearly drown in swollen rivers, did you?'

'No,' Jim said. 'As a matter of fact I didn't.'

She fixed him with a demanding stare. 'So why *did* you come?'

'I am looking for a City,' he told her, matching her stare with his own.

'Raaark? What? Out here? What kind of City?'

He stood, a little unsteady at first due to the water in his ears, and went and took his knapsack and sleeping blanket from the branch. 'I, too, have a book,' he said, sitting again. He opened the knapsack and took out the old green leather-bound volume with its scrawny black feather bookmark. 'ChaCha Muchos, they call it,' he said, showing the bird the engraving. 'The Lost City of the Dancers.'

'Ha, ha, ha! Creeeaaark! Ha, ha, ha, ha, ha, ha, ha!' The bird was hopping up and down, laughing so much she was almost splitting her feathers.

'What's so funny?' asked Jim, closing the book and fearing the worst.

'Ha, ha, ha *ha*!' Small tears ran down her beak

and she was holding her belly with both wings. '*That* is,' she spluttered.

'What?'

'The City doesn't look like *that*!' she scoffed derisively. 'Oh my beak, no!'

Cairo Jim went very still, so still that his heart almost stopped working. At that moment the jungle on the other side of the Marjangower River became *absolutely silent*. It was as though the world over there with all its leaves and mosquitoes and vines and trees had skipped a beat.

'You know of it?' he asked, the hope building in his voice.

'Reeaaarark! You bet your bootstraps!'

Jim's forehead was glistening. 'Do you know the way there?'

She answered him in a low squawk. 'Every year I follow the Indians as they traverse this steep mountain on their annual pilgrimage to this place. I have been there many times.'

'You do know the way!'

'Raark!'

Jim clasped his hands tightly together. 'Oh, please, will you guide me there? I will make it worth your while.'

She puffed out her chest feathers and looked at him carefully. He *did* seem different to all the others who had come here. He *did* have a thoughtful step (except when he went skidding), and a kind face, and hands not meant for barbarism. And his pith helmet was most definitely of the jaunty variety.

'I will give you my answer,' she replied in a voice

neither hopeful nor despairing, 'on the morrow. Until then you will rest.'

She shot off and pulled his umbrella out from the bank. 'Here,' she said, dropping it softly beside him. 'Stick this in the ground for shelter—such a strange contraption—and sleep for tonight.'

She was right. Jim's eyes were growing heavy. 'Yes, all right then,' he mumbled, putting the book away. 'Today *has* been somewhat exhausting. Archaeology was never meant——'

'And your little life is rounded with a sleep.'

'By the way, my name's Jim. Cairo Jim.' He yawned, his mouth stretched so wide that he could have swallowed his own head. 'I'm an——'

'I know what you are,' she squawked peacefully as his eyes closed. 'I have seen inside your leather sack...'

And slowly the darkness started to fall and breathe and swell about them, and all the while the clever bird kept watch over it all.

Jim woke the next morning to the sounds of a brand new, screeching, twittering, chattering day.

During the night the macaw must have taken the sleeping blanket from his knapsack and rolled it up for a pillow, for he now found his head resting comfortably on it. He sat up, stretched out his arms and, with a half yawn, slowly inhaled the invigorating air.

There was a beating of wings in the leaves behind, and there she was, hovering in the air in front of him with one wing, the other wrapped around a hefty calabash gourd.

'Raark!' she greeted him. 'Good morning, Cairo Jim.'

'Good morning to you,' he smiled.

'Methinks you slept well.'

'Yes,' he said, rubbing his eyes. 'I feel most refreshed.'

'That is good.' She fluttered to the ground and laid the calabash gourd in front of him. It was hollowed out and filled with small purple berries. 'Something to start you,' she squawked.

'Thank you,' Jim said. He seized the gourd and began tucking in with his fingers.

'Raark! No, use this.' She tossed him a lustrous leaf which was shaped low in the middle and higher at the sides and which resembled a simple trowel. The stalk of the leaf even made a good handle. 'Scoop them up with that, or else the juice will stain your hands for days.'

'Thank you.'

The berries tasted juicy and good, although a little prickly on the tongue. The macaw blinked as she watched him eating.

After a few mouthfuls he looked up at her and asked if she would guide him to the City.

'Devour your meal,' she replied, 'and I shall tell you something. A story you need to know.'

'A story?'

'The story of the ChaCha Muchonians. How they came to be, and how they came not to be. And then I will ask *you* something.'

He listened intently to her as he munched. Some of the things she told him he already knew from the

Old Relics Society book, but they had been only a small fragment of the whole story. What in fact she told him in her chirping resonances was exactly the same tale Zapateado had told young Yupichu: how Sandra Panza and the Cuzconian rebels had been found by the ancient tribe of Indians, how Arturo Murrayo and his people had led them up to the pinnacle of HokeyCokey Mountain, how they had carved out the City, and then, in more sombre tones, how Sandra Panza, the maker of the famous Cuzco Clackersmackers, had descended into her dreadful state and plummeted to her destiny.

As the bird recounted each incident she became more and more animated in the telling of it all, her wings opening and folding about her, her voice going from squawk-growl to excited, jumpy screech.

'And so,' she said, 'after Arturo Murrayo had the dream, every year the Indians went up the Mountain to await Her return from Her great height, when She would bring Her music back with Her. And every year *my* ancestors have followed them, undercover in the treetops. So far She has not come back, but the Indians have not given up hope. They are sure they will find Her again.'

Cairo Jim had finished the berries. He put down the gourd and wiped his lips with the outside of the leaf. 'My goodness,' he said. 'I had no idea there was so much to it.'

The macaw hopped up and down. 'There are many stories out here,' she squawked. 'You would be surprised.'

'How do you come to know it all?'

'From listening.'

'To whom?'

'To an old Indian. I was in a tree only recently when he told it to a young Indian on the other side of the river. I remembered it as he told it.' She stretched her neck and ruffled the feathers under her beak. 'Birds have very good memories for words,' she cooed. 'That's why human beings often teach us how to talk.'

'Well, plant me in the sand and call me an obelisk,' said Cairo Jim. He stood and stretched his legs. Then he turned to her. 'So. Will you please take me there?' he asked.

'First I must ask you a question. If your answer satisfies me, I will be your guide. Otherwise, adios, senor.'

Jim looked at her earnestly. 'Ask away,' he said.

She puffed out her chest feathers and blinked. 'Why do you want to find this place? What do you hope to find there that is so valuable to you? Is it gold? Jewels? Clackersmackers? If so, you're wasting my time.'

'No,' he replied. 'None of those. There *is* something I want, but it's not anything you can hold in your hand or put in a box or even eat. What I want is *knowledge*.'

The bird blinked rapidly and made a sort of brrerk-ing sound.

'You've just told me that the ChaCha Muchonians danced themselves to extinction, that a whole race of people became no more. I need to know *how* and *why* they disappeared. You see,' he rubbed his chin, 'they were human beings too. They lived and breathed just like my race does today, although they danced more prodigiously. It's in the interests not only of archaeology, but also of the *future*, that I try to find out why they went into decline. There must have been something happening at that time which made them act in this obsessive manner. Something which affected them. Maybe if we could find the reason, the cause of it all, we might be able to prevent it from happening to the human species ever again.'

'Is your species worth so much?' the bird asked, her small eyes glinting.

'Not all of us are bad,' said Jim.

'What kind of thing do you hope to find to give you this reason, this knowledge?'

'I don't know,' he frowned. 'I won't know until I get there and find it. Maybe some ancient document carefully preserved...'

'Raaark! They didn't keep documents. They recorded everything by tying knots in pieces of rope.'

'Oh,' said Jim. 'Well, maybe there's something else...'

From the brightness of his eyes the bird could see his desire was intense. 'And if you find the reason?' she prowked. 'What will you do then?'

'Then I shall go back to the Old Relics Society in Cairo and write it up and have it published in the Society newsletter, perhaps with a nice poem to go with it. And maybe archaeologists and other humans will take notice of these findings, and maybe this terrible thing won't happen again.'

Silence followed, during which Jim stood with his hands in his pockets and stared at the sky. To the bird he seemed a long way away. She thought carefully about what he had said, and the way he had said it, and she concluded that he was a bird of a feather.

'All right!' she screeched. 'Cairo Jim, your reason is admirable to me! Tell me when you wish to leave, and I will take you there!'

He felt as though someone had let off a sky-rocket up his back. So excited was he, he did an involuntary little jig on the grass. The bird cackled and joined him in her own plumpish waddling manner.

'How about right now?' he shouted.

'It shall be so,' she cried. 'Gather your things and we will begin.'

He quickly began strapping his sleeping blanket onto his knapsack and tidying himself up. 'You still haven't told me about your book,' he said to her.

'Rark. I'll do better than that. I'll show it to you. We will be going by the spot where I keep it. It is on our way to the City.'

'I can hardly wait,' said Jim. He hoisted the knapsack onto his shoulders, fastened his scabbard to his belt, put his binoculars and compass around his neck, and gave his umbrella a good shake before closing it.

'That's odd,' he said, looking around the grass.

'What is the bother?' asked the bird.

'My pith helmet. It was here last night, but now...'

The bird shot off into the foliage and returned with the hat hanging from her beak by its chinstrap. It was as white as the day it had been made.

'For the love of Rameses,' gasped Jim.

'I cleaned it in the night,' she said, dropping it

into his hands. 'We have many wonderful cleansers in our jungle mud.'

'Thank you,' he said, very touched.

'And now, let us make tracks.' She fluttered ahead of him.

'Wait!' he called after her as she disappeared out of the clearing. 'Have you got a name?'

'I am a macaw,' she screeched back. 'What's in a name? We don't have them. Keep up or I'll lose you!'

'Then I shall call you Doris,' said Cairo Jim, hurrying to catch up with her. 'Because that is what you look like.'

9

THE DAWNING OF DOLORES DEL TEMPO

CROUCHED in the cool dark ferns, dawdling far behind his tribe, Yupichu heard it.

He froze and listened, his heart beating like a metronome. It was a long way off, but there was no doubt about it; soaring along on the steamy air of the calm jungle evening, soaring like a sound from some muffled yesterday, soaring through the leaves and vines and ancient boughs, *he could hear music.*

It was as sweet to his ears as honey to a bee.

He would show them. He would do it. He was ripening. With barely a sound he gathered his sleeping bundle and fastened it to his waistcloth. Then he picked up his spear and set off, creeping like a jaguar through the jungle twilight.

*　　*　　*

At the Bone–von Mostetot–del Tempo camp the evening was engulfed by the piercing scream of melody.

'Ah, listen, amiga.' Mendoza smiled at the dozing camel sitting near the paraffin lamp. 'Such peachy rhythm, si?'

The beast stirred in her snorting slumber and fluttered her eyelashes.

'She is a hugely talented senorita, that one. So clever. Sometimes when she is playing at the Popocatepetl Club, I get so excited my hands shake and I cannot keep the spotlight still enough. Of course, I tell her it goes wobbly because she is so tall and I cannot light the whole of her at the one time. If I told her the real reason why it goes wobbly, she would think me a complete fool, si?'

The camel snored quietly, oblivious to the screechy high-pitched notes coming from the jungle.

'One day,' he whispered, 'she will see me as I *truly* am...you wait and see.' He straightened his hair and smiled to himself.

Neptune Bone stumbled out of Dolores's tentette (where he had been poking about in her make-up collection, trying to find her manicure kit). He was wearing his Prussian Blue fez with the Primrose Yellow tassel and his hands were clamped firmly over his ear holes. 'Arrrr! What is that demonic din?'

'It is Miss del Tempo,' answered Mendoza, eyeing him suspiciously.

'What is it she is strangling?' grimaced the bearded man.

'Oh, no, senor, she is not strangling anything——'

'She is murdering the very night! Arrrr!'

'Oh, no, that is her violin.'

'What?'

'Si, I tuned it myself.'

'You jest, Mendoza. Not even you could do such a bad job. I think Madam is wrestling with a howling hobgoblin, and the unfortunate creature is most definitely losing.'

'Oh, no, Senor von Mostetot. That is "Burly Keith's Lament".'

'What?'

'The song she is playing. It is called "Burly Keith's Lament". Burly Keith, you see, is a sailor, a man of the seas, who has left his lovely Lana behind. It is a very sad song. Listen, I will sing it for you.'

'No, I'd rather you——'

Mendoza took a deep breath and began singing along to the screech:

> The gulls have flit
> across the sea,
> you used to spit
> but not at me,
> this shipwrecked heart of mine is yearning:
> Lana, where can you be? Eeeeeeee.

'All right,' rumbled Bone, 'I get the idea.'

> When I remember how you used to lick my
>   tattoos so
> —I'm so burly—
> how you snorted 'gainst my chest, and all I did
>   was go.
> Oh, Lana, you're so girly. . .

'Desist!' cried Bone. 'Stop now and I'll give you a bauble!'

The ocean's tears,
the albatross,
your perfumed ears,
your sweet lip gloss,
this flotsammed heart of mine is churning:
llama, please wait for me. Eeeeeeee...

'Arrrr! That's it! No more! I can't bear it!'

'What about another verse, senor? There are only nineteen more to go before it gets *really* tragic.'

'No, you tone-deaf little man. I'd rather pick all the fleas off Desdemona with my bare teeth than listen to more of *that*.'

Mendoza looked at him even more suspiciously than before. At that moment there was a sharp *ping* from the darkness, followed by a loud growl.

'What was that?' whispered Bone, his eyes wide.

'Oh, do not fear. It is just Miss del Tempo. She has broken a string again. Maybe I tuned it too tightly.'

'At least it'll stop her torturing us.'

'Oh, it takes more than that to stop her. Sometimes she plays at the Popocatepetl Club with only *one* string.'

'Merciful Heavens!'

'Si, that is what I thought the first time I heard her.' He took a deep breath and sighed loudly once again. 'And in all the time since then my amazement for her has not waned one little candle flicker.'

'Hrrrmph.'

'Senor, I will tell you something. I think that it is because of her great talents that so many men have tried to deceive her by pretending they are Princes and

Counts and Barons. Some people like to be surrounded by such great talent, and they will stop at nothing to achieve this.'

Bone lit a fat cigar. 'I'd rather be surrounded by a carousel of caterwauling choirboys scraping their fingernails against some almighty blackboard,' he puffed.

'Ah, but we have seen the last of those scoundrels, Senor von Mostetot. At least I hope so.' Mendoza began to go very red in the cheeks. 'Why, if I found anyone deceiving Miss del Tempo again by pretending to be something he is not, by the Mother Earth I would break every bone——'

'Yes?' said Bone, who was only vaguely listening.

'I said every bone——'

'What do you want?'

'Every bone——'

'*Well?*'

'——in his deceiving body.'

Bone held the cigar between his clenched teeth and inspected his fingernails carefully. 'Oh, this place,' he moaned. 'The sooner Madam gets us to the City, the better. I certainly hope she knows where we're going. There have been times during the last couple of weeks when I've thought she's been leading us all on a wild ibis chase.'

'She knows where she's heading, have no fear.'

'I hope so,' he said in a low and sinister voice.

All at once the music stopped and they heard a huge crashing of bush and tree.

'What was that?' hissed Bone.

'Quaao?' snorted the camel, awakened by the commotion.

There was a blur of height and colour and speed, and into the clearing burst Dolores del Tempo.

'Aargh!' she wailed, her violin shaking by her side. 'That was close.'

'What happened, Miss del Tempo?'

'Something...something *got* me!'

There was a rocketing *craaark* from the forest, which made the hair on the back of Bone's neck stand on end. Mendoza led the trembling senorita to a rock, where she sat and fanned her face with a droopy lace handkerchief. Her red frilly dress still trembled.

'What was it?' asked Mendoza.

'I do not know,' she gasped. 'There I am, fiddling away by myself in the moonlight, building to a crescendo of great sadness for Burly Keith, when from the dark forest floor I suddenly feel my toes being got at. "Thunk, thunk, thunk!" I hear. And then my toes curl up and I jump high into the night, so high, Mendoza, that I fling out my arm and grab hold of a very tall branch. I hang onto it tightly, my violin under my other arm, and I look down to the blackness on the ground to try and see this attacking thing.'

'What was there?'

She lowered her voice. 'All I see are two slits, as red as the sunset on a hot day, looking up at me. Then the next moment the blackness smothers them, and I hear a cackle, a croaking cackle unlike any human sound, and then all is silence.'

'Idiot bird,' thought Bone.

'That is when I let go of the branch and fall to the ground. Then I vamoose all the way back here.

Oh, what an ordeal! What a fright!' She grabbed Mendoza by the shoulders. 'Look at me.'

'Si, Miss del Tempo, I am looking.' His heart fluttered.

'How many more wrinkles do I have because of my ordeal?'

Mendoza opened his mouth to reply when she rose abruptly and pushed him away. 'Oh, never mind. You would be too kind to give me a truthful answer!' She brushed past him and disappeared into her tentette.

'Senorita?' he called after her.

'Arrr, let her go,' grumbled Bone. 'There's nothing——'

There he stopped, and there Mendoza's eyes widened in alarm, because there in front of them, at the edge of the clearing, a large bush was shaking wildly.

'Look, Senor von Mostetot, something is in there!'

Bone sighed and blew a shaft of smoke out of the corner of his mouth. 'Desdemona!' he called. 'Stop cavorting about and come over here. I want a manicure.'

The bush shook in reply, its leaves rustling loudly.

'Desdemona? Come out of there this instant!'

The raven swooped in from behind and perched on top of Bone's fez. 'Craark. Come out of where?'

'What were you doing in that bush?'

'What bush? I was in no bush. I was out giving the frightful fiddler a scare, not lurking about in any bush.'

'Don't lie to me, bird.'

'Craark, who's lying? I'm telling——'

The bush shook again, more violently than ever.

'Raark, I'm off!' cried Desdemona, shooting up into the darkness.

'Quaaoo!' snorted the camel, rising and moving well clear.

Bone grabbed Mendoza and held the small man in front of him like a shield. 'Mendoza, you must protect me,' he ordered. 'Without me this expedition would not be. You must not let that savage thing in there—oh, no, I'm too young to go to the Underworld just yet!'

The middle branches of the bush shook and parted, and out stepped a hot-eyed Yupichu, his grey hair wild and tangled, his spear at the ready.

'By Thoth, it's a native!' cried Bone.

Yupichu stayed glued where he was, staring unblinkingly at the overdressed Bone and the mat-headed Mendoza and the animal that looked like a llama with lumps.

'Mendoza,' Bone whispered, 'go into my tent-pavilion. In my trunk you will find a stack of photographs of myself. Do not pause to admire them, but extricate one and bring it back to me. And hurry!'

Mendoza looked at Yupichu, then at Bone, then at Yupichu again. Then he grabbed the camel's bridle and both of them dashed into the tent-pavilion.

Bone took a step towards the boy, who immediately took a step backwards.

Bone removed his fez. 'Good evening,' he smirked lopsidedly, a small breeze wafting a pruney smell off his shoulders.

Yupichu looked up at him through his thick brows.

The man was dressed in a way Yupichu had never beheld. What a strange part of the jungle this was.

'Do not fear, I will not exploit you.'

Yupichu held his spear in both hands, pointing it at Bone. 'Where is She?' he hissed.

'You speak my language?' The smoke billowed down through his nostrils.

'Our Awaited. She came this way. What have you done with Her?'

'Your *what*?'

'She has music. I hear it in the forest. She has brought Her music back with Her.'

Captain Neptune Bone's eyes gleamed through the smoke. He dropped his cigar to the ground and stubbed it out quickly. 'Oh, yes, She has,' he said quietly, curious to find out what the boy meant. 'She has indeed.'

'Zapateado said She would one day come back from Her great height, and tonight I have seen it. Before my very eyes She fell from the heavens to the darkness of the ground. She played Her music and fell from the skies. Now I must take Her to my people.' Yupichu looked warily around the camp, still keeping his spear aimed at Bone's stomach. 'Tell me where She is, so that I may lead Her to the City.'

The large man gasped, and gripped his fez tightly. 'The. . .City?' he whispered.

'Si. I must take Sandra of the Heavens there *now*.'

'Sandra of the Heavens?'

'Our Awaited,' he nodded solemnly.

Something clicked then in Bone's head, and his devious, scheming brain turned full-circle. 'Arrr, of course,' he smiled, throwing his arms wide open. 'Your Sandra is returning to the City! And that is where your people are?'

'Si,' grunted Yupichu. 'That is where we go every year to wait for Her. Every year since we have built ChaCha Muchos we have gone back to wait.'

A dizziness began to overwhelm Bone, and through the sensation he recalled what Desdemona had quoted from the Old Relics Society book. It was as if the words were etched into his brain in gold-leaf lettering: *'It is said they stumbled across an ancient Indian tribe who possessed a rare and hitherto unknown potion... capable of dissolving every substance known...except leather...a small gourd of this potion...used to carve out their city...high atop a foliage-covered mountain.'*

Then the dizziness evaporated and in his mind he saw the vast doors of the great Cairo Museum. He could almost smell the gold behind them.

'Where is She?' the boy demanded.

Neptune Bone snapped back to the wonderful reality before him. 'Oh, She is here, do not worry,' he purred. 'I know where She is.' He extended his hand. 'You see, *I* am her Guardian, Otto of the Heavens.'

Yupichu looked puzzled.

'Yes,' continued Bone, '*I* have brought your Sandra here, where we knew we would find you. And now you must take us to your people.'

At that moment Dolores emerged from her tentette, holding her handkerchief over her nose. 'Phew!' she snorted. 'It smells like rotting prunes in there!'

Yupichu let out a howl of awe. He dropped to his knees and lowered his head. 'Welcome, Celestial One,' he breathed. 'Welcome, Our Awaited!'

'Who is this?' asked Dolores, unsure what to make of the tousle-haired, ancient-looking youth.

'This, Madam, is our salvation.'

'What?'

'I come,' said Yupichu, raising his head and allowing himself only the slightest glimpse of her, 'to lead You to Your people.'

'My people?' said Dolores.

Bone put his hand beside his mouth and whispered. 'They are at the City now. They are, I believe, descendants of the tribe who built the place.'

A small shiver surged up and down Dolores's spine. She knew only too well what this meant, and the implication was quite delicious. Keeping her dark eyes fixed on Yupichu, she straightened herself to her full, empowering height.

She smiled. 'You don't say?'

'Oh, I do, I do,' Bone almost sang. 'Arrr, I certainly do.'

'My people have waited for You for many seasons,' said Yupichu, rising slowly. 'More than even Zapateado remembers, and he is the Keeper of the Past.'

'I do not understand,' frowned Dolores.

Bone shushed her. 'You do not *have* to understand, Madam. *I* know what to do.' He stepped towards Yupichu again, and this time the boy did not retreat. 'My dear boy, it has been a long journey from the Heavens for us all, and there is still a fair way to go to the top of the Mountain. Blast!' He swatted at a mosquito. 'Our Sandra must have Her celestial shut-eye tonight, and then first thing in the morning you must lead us all onwards to your people.'

'Our Sandra?' said Dolores.

'I'll explain later,' muttered Bone.

'Si,' said Yupichu. 'She must rest. She must be refreshed for Her arrival.'

'What is your name, boy?' asked Bone.

Yupichu lowered his spear very, very slowly. 'Yupichu,' he answered, unable to take his eyes from Dolores.

'What a strange, wizened thing you are. Come.' Bone took him by the arm and led him to the door of Dolores's tentette. 'There is a comfy patch of earth here where you may keep guard over our Sandra. Make sure nothing dastardly happens to her in the night. Tomorrow we shall set off bright and early.'

Mendoza rushed out of the tent-pavilion, his hair awry, waving a photograph in the air. 'Here it is, Senor von Mostetot. It took me some time to find it. I did not recognise you in all that gold braid and feathers.'

Bone snatched the picture from him and thrust it at Yupichu. 'Here, boy,' he said, as though he were handing him a great treat. 'A little gift. Something to treasure.'

Yupichu looked at the portrait, then put it down on his patch of dirt and plonked himself on top of it so that he was sitting on the bearded one's head.

'Arrr,' Bone sneered, and, turning on his heel, went to his tent-pavilion.

Mendoza looked at Dolores. 'Miss del Tempo, what is happening?'

'I am not exactly sure,' she replied, stepping over the adoring, yawning boy and entering her tentette. 'But one thing I know: we are certainly on our way. Goodnight, Mendoza. Goodnight, Yupichu.' She closed the door-flap and disappeared from them.

'Goodnight, senorita,' frowned Mendoza. He looked at the boy, already curled up and fast asleep. Then he fetched his blanket and went over to the camel, whom Bone had shunted discourteously out of his tent-pavilion. Together they bedded down and waited for the coming dawn.

10

To an Ancient Civilisation

CAIRO Jim and Doris the macaw travelled along a narrow trail which every day took them higher and higher up HokeyCokey Mountain.

They passed through mighty arches of branches as heavy as the sky; they wandered by ferns as huge as elephants; they ducked underneath waterfalls as pure and clear as the freshest glacial ice, and for much of their journey they talked.

'Do you have many friends?' she asked him on the third day.

'A few,' he replied. 'Not as many as some people. Most of the time I keep to myself in the Valley of the Kings. But the friends I have are good friends. There's Gerald Perry Esquire, who sent me on this expedition. He's a founding member of the Old Relics Society, and always manages to find enough money to keep funding my work. He's very kind, and very encouraging. And there's Miss Jocelyn Osgood. I have her picture in my knapsack. You almost met her the day we were in that "noisy metallic bird".'

Doris was fluttering a little way ahead. She stopped for a moment and perched on a huge, glistening frond, waiting for him to catch up. 'Is she an archaeologist also?' she prowked.

'No,' said Jim, puffing along. 'She works for Valkyrian Airways as a flight attendant. I've known her for a while. Some people think she's bossy, I don't know why.' He took out his handkerchief and wiped his forehead. 'There's also a camel named Brenda. I met her only recently. She keeps me company in the Valley.'

'Does she talk?'

Jim looked at her in a strange manner. 'Of course not. She's a camel, for goodness' sake.'

'Is she still there, in the Valley?' asked Doris, fluttering off again but still listening.

His pace slackened for a moment and he sighed. 'I really don't know. She vanished shortly before I left. Maybe she wanted to go back to her herd. . .' Then he picked up his rhythm and began marching along again. 'Doris?'

'Raark?'

'Do *you* have many friends?'

There was a short silence before she spoke. 'No. Not many. ''You cannot tell who's your friend'', as the great man himself once wrote. I *know* a lot of birds—toucans, condors, Amazonian double-speckled wartwarblers—and I sometimes mix with the other macaws, but I wouldn't count them as *friends*. The macaws would rather spend their time sucking mud from the riverbank, a very uncivilised thing to do.'

'Why do they do it?'

'To fix their bellies. They eat too much fruit and they get upset bellies. By sucking mud it makes them better. Something in the mud, I'm not sure what.'

'And you don't indulge in such activity?'

'I don't need to. I prefer to eat snails rather than fruit. But I prefer most of all to read my book, all alone, without all that noise and raucousness. The man in white said that was the best way to read, and he was right.'

Jim wanted to ask her more about the man in white and about the book, but suddenly he found it quite difficult to breathe. It was as though the air was coming through a thick invisible handkerchief, and no matter how much he tried to gulp it down, he could hardly inhale. 'Doris?' he called.

'Reerk! What?'

'Why is it so hard to breathe?'

She circled and came back to him. 'Ah. I was wondering how long it would take before it affected you. We are reaching higher altitude.'

'Really?' he gasped.

'The air is thinner. And it'll get thinner the more we climb. Be not afraid, you won't suffer if you go a bit slower. Take a good, slow pace, and breathe as deeply as you can with every second step. Come on.' Off she flew.

'Doris?'

'Reraark?' She stopped and hovered above the trail, looking back at him.

'Do you mind if we stop for a few minutes? I'm——'

'Screeeeaaaark! Don't touch that tree!'

She torpedoed back and hovered between him and the tall, thin tree trunk he was about to lean against.

'Why ever not?' he asked, trembling from her sudden outburst.

'This is why ever not. Behold its bark!'

The archaeologist–poet looked carefully. It did not appear out of the ordinary; to him it was only a tall, thin tree trunk. Then his eyes picked out something strange.

There was a line running along the vertical of the tree, all the way from the top right down to where it entered the earth. It was a slender brown line, no wider than a needle, and it was *moving*. Only ever so slightly, but most definitely moving. Jim craned his neck to get a closer look.

'Fire ants,' squawked Doris.

'Fire ants?'

'Rark. The most lethal ants in all the jungle. If you get bitten by a fire ant, for weeks you feel as if a burning stick is being held against your skin, and there is nothing you can do to relieve it. No amount of water or palm leaves or cool mud will lessen the sting. You must wait in agony until time will one day end it.'

'My goodness.'

'Many years ago, men came into this forest and up this mountain searching for gold. They found none, so instead they captured local Indians and tied them to trees such as this.'

'The Indians would have died in agony,' said Jim.

'Yes. How humans can do that sort of thing to their own kind, I do not know. . .'

'Come on,' Jim said, shuddering. 'Let's go. I very much want to see this book you squawk of.'

She looked at him and let out a small screech. Then her eyes creased around the edges and, with a happier beat in her wings, she again led the way upwards and onwards.

Towards nightfall they came to a dip in the trail. They followed this down to a place where it opened into a small, grassy clearing bordered by a circle of thick, gnarled, vine-covered trees. A branch from one of these trees extended right out into the centre of the clearing, and hanging from this branch was a long, knotted vine. On the end of the vine dangled a large bundle of leaves.

Doris flew down onto the soft grass. 'Raark. Here we shall stay for tonight. It is well protected and you should be most comfortable.'

Jim looked around and felt quite safe and secluded. He slung off his knapsack and took a long swig from his water bottle, which he had filled at the last waterfall. 'Heavens, I'm exhausted,' he puffed, sitting heavily.

'Then you should rest,' said the macaw. She opened her wings and closed them around herself, stretching her scapular feathers before they began to get stiff. 'I'll fly off and gather some food. Will fruit be to your liking?'

'Thank you,' said Jim, taking off his pith helmet and wiping his neck. 'That would be most——'

'Rightio.' And before he could blink she was off.

While she was gone he lay back and closed his eyes. The journey so far had taken much longer than either he or Gerald Perry Esquire had anticipated, but despite the few mishaps he was still feeling fit and healthy, and his spirits were good, thanks largely to his new feathered companion. The more they had journeyed, the stronger his desire had become to find out what had happened to the ChaCha Muchonians. *Why* did they disappear the way they had? What was the cause? How long, he wondered, would it be before he and Doris walked (and flew) through the gates of the City? If only he knew when they would arrive...

He opened his eyes and put his hands behind his head. Straight above him the large bundle of leaves was swinging gently back and forth in the breeze. It was an odd looking bundle—not round like a big nut, nor long and clumpy like a leafy bunch of bananas, nor oval like a calabash gourd. It looked unnatural for the jungle, and he could not help thinking the leaves were concealing something.

Just then there was a whoop-whoop-whoop of air, and Doris was hovering above him with one wing, while the other was scooped around a cluster of oranges, bananas and berries. She dropped them gently onto the grass near him.

'Do nothing but eat, and make good cheer, and praise heaven for the merry year,' she sang.

Jim sat up and looked at her admiringly. 'That's very good, Doris,' he said, reaching for an orange. 'Very poetic.'

'Rerk. Thank you. I had a good teacher,' she prowked, letting her breast feathers ruffle. 'The best ever.'

'Who was that?' munched Jim. 'The man in white?'

She moved her head and neck up and down three

or four times. 'No, not him. Although he led me to my teacher.'

'Who, then?'

'Light a fire and I will show you.'

He was puzzled, but unable to resist her offer, he stood and went to collect some dry wood.

Soon he had built a large pile of branches, twigs, and dead fronds and set a match to it. In little more than a minute the pile was blazing steadily, lighting up the fading day.

'Now go and sit again,' she instructed. 'In the same place as before.'

He did as he was told. Away she darted to an old tree opposite him. A little way up, at a point where a fat, sweeping branch grew, she stopped and perched in the gloomy cleft between branch and trunk. She lowered her head and poked about with her mandible on the other side of the branch.

Jim saw a long vine wriggling about against the bark and he realised that the bird was untying the vine.

At last she had it free. With the end firmly clamped in her beak she began to ascend, very carefully. As she did so, the bundle of leaves began to descend very slowly, until it came to rest on the lush grass beside Jim.

When it was safely settled she let go of the vine and fluttered down to join it.

'The best hiding place in the world,' she screeched. 'The only people who pass by here are the Indians once a year on their way up to the City. They've either never seen it, or think it's some kind of weird fruit. Either way, they've always left it alone, and it's always been untouched. A good thing, too. I really can't imagine what I'd do if it were spoilt.'

Her squawk had become excited as she bent low over the bundle. With infinite care, she used her beak to untie the vine from around it. It was fastened in roughly the same manner as straps on a satchel. When the vine was loose she draped it elegantly on the grass, then proceeded to peel off the thick, rubbery leaves one by one.

Jim watched all this keenly, anxious to know what lay beneath.

Finally she pulled away the last leaf. 'Here is my legacy,' she announced.

'Why,' gasped Jim, 'it's a book.'

'*The* book,' warbled the macaw.

The archaeologist–poet stared down at a thick, aged volume with dusky brown leather covers and yellowing pages. On the front cover a head-and-shoulders portrait of a man was embossed in bright yellow gold. He had a balding head, with long hair covering his ears, and a little moustache and goatee. His eyes held a cheeky wisdom, and the collar he wore was from a time long past.

Cairo Jim recognised him at once.

'Mr Shakespeare,' he gasped.

'Methought you would know him,' squawked Doris happily.

'Goodness, I've known him since I was a small boy. Doris, do you mind if I have a look inside?'

'Be my guest.'

He picked up the book as though it were a cobweb (as Doris knew he would) and opened its heavy covers.

On the title page he read (printed in bold, fancy letters and old-fashioned spelling):

MR WILLIAM SHAKESPEARES
COMEDIES,
HISTORIES,
TRAGEDIES,
SONNETS, & POEMS.
Publifhed according to the True Originall Copies.
LONDON 1623

'It's a first edition,' prowked the macaw.

'Well, I'll be...where on earth did you find it?'

She was waddling about and hopping up and down, excited that after so long she could share her treasure with someone else who understood her thrill. 'From the man in white,' she screeched. 'He brought it with him when he came into the forest. When the great silver bird came and took him away, he made a gift of it to me.'

'What a gift!'

'Raark! You said it, matey! Do you like Senor Shakespeare?'

'I'll say,' replied Jim, leafing through the pages. 'He was perhaps the greatest writer ever...'

Doris nodded her head and squawked. 'I knew it,' she flapped, 'I knew you would understand! There was something about you the first time I laid eyes on you which made me think, "He knows Senor Shakespeare". That is why I took you under my wing. Reeerraaarrk!'

Then, until the night became unfathomably dark, they screeched and talked and squawked and chatted about their favourite scenes from the great writer's plays. They laughed as they remembered Pistol and the Fool and Bottom and Belch; they recalled how they had trembled at the great tempest raging about King Lear, and at the appearance of the ghost of Hamlet's father on the castle battlements, and at the haggishly hideous witches on the battle field in Scotland. So enthusiastic was their discussion, such fun were they having, that Jim forgot all about his supper which still lay ripe and neglected next to him.

'Doris,' he said at one point. 'I've just had a thought. Do you realise that Mr Shakespeare was writing his plays and sonnets at about the same time in history as the creation of ChaCha Muchos was taking place?'

She became still and gazed wide-eyed into the fire. 'Well, well, well,' she clucked quietly. She turned to Jim and the edges of her eyes wrinkled. 'There must have been great rhythm in the world back then.'

'Yes,' said Jim, beginning to think again of the City. 'And somewhere along the line, somewhere up on this Mountain, it skipped a beat.' He frowned and yawned.

'It is time for sleep,' she squawked. 'You must have all the rest you can, for tomorrow you will need every bit of your energy if we are to reach the Moongate in good time.'

'The Moongate?'

'Raark. The Moongate. It is high in the cliff. From it you will see ChaCha Muchos above.'

A huge outbreak of goosebumps took hold of Cairo Jim. 'And how far,' he asked, his voice trembly, 'how far is it from the Moongate to the City itself?'

'Uphill all the way, a hop, skip and flutter. Which is macawspeak for two human hours. Now good night. I shall be in the leaves if you need me.'

She raised her wings, but stopped before they were above her head. 'Cairo Jim?'

'Yes, Doris?'

'Please would you put Senor Shakespeare in your sack? I should like to take him with us to the City.'

'By all means.' He carefully slid the book into his knapsack, where it rested snugly against the Old Relics Society volume.

'Gracias. Until the morrow.' She bowed her head, gave a small screech, and, like an inverted parachute, rose into the leafy darkness above.

'Until the morrow,' said Cairo Jim, and then, much more quietly to himself, 'and what a day it will be.'

11

MENDOZA DROPS A BUNDLE

'Arrr,' grimaced Bone, sitting high atop the long-suffering camel. 'That boy is leading us at a cracking pace. I'm glad I'm not walking.'

'Craark,' croaked Desdemona, perched on his shoulder. 'That'll be the day! The oceans of the world will burn dry before you go walking anywhere.'

'Idiot bird. If I weren't finding it so difficult to breathe I'd swipe at you here and now.'

'Nevermore!' She pecked at a chomping flea.

'Si,' nodded Dolores del Tempo breathlessly as she swayed back and forth on the nether hump. 'I, too, am having trouble getting my breath.'

'It is the height,' puffed Mendoza, barely visible under his hugeous load as he hurried to catch up with the lurching beast. 'The air up here is rarefied. You will find it much harder to breathe unless you are used to the atmosphere.'

'*He* seems used to it,' Bone sneered, looking ahead at the fast-moving boy. He pulled his megaphone from the camel's saddlebag and raised it to his fleshly lips. 'Yupichu!' he bellowed. 'How far is it now?'

Yupichu slowed down and looked back over his shoulder. 'We reach the Moongate very soon.'

'How soon?'

'In one day and a half. Are you travelling well, Our Awaited?'

'Si,' frowned Dolores, dabbing at her face with her lacy handkerchief.

'Soon, when You are with us again in our midst, everything will be all right.'

'And how far,' Bone bellowed, 'is the City from the Moongate?'

'A short distance.'

'*How* short?'

'About two hours by foot. But for you, maybe six hours.'

'Ha!' snorted the large man. 'The beast will do it quicker than that!'

'Oh, no,' said Yupichu, beginning to hurry again. 'The path from the Moongate is too narrow for anyone to ride her. She must walk alone.'

'*What?*' Bone's voice thundered metallically.

'Si. If she were to carry you, she might overbalance and tumble off the cliff. It is a long way down to the Marjangower River, and its waters are cruel and crushing.'

'Quaaoo,' came a happy snort.

'Blast!' Bone cursed. He was about to call something else to Yupichu, but the nimble youth rounded the corner and for the moment was gone. Bone glared angrily ahead.

'Phew,' panted Mendoza, the perspiration dripping from his forehead. 'All this fuss about one tiny mountainous City! Who would have ever thought such interest could be aroused? And fancy that after so long, with no-one bothering to even breathe the name of ChaCha Muchos, *two* people should want to find it. How peculiar. Phew!'

'What is all this stultiloquence?' growled Bone. He turned to the streaming man. 'What are you babbling about, Wonky-hair?'

'Well,' he puffed, 'it is strange to me that you and that archaeologist senor should want at the same time to go and find the City. Coincidence, eh, Senor von Mostetot?'

Neptune Bone began to go very cold. He whispered as though his voice was a cutlass. 'What do you mean, *archaeologist*?'

'He came to the Popocatepetl Club not long before you. Asking Miss del Tempo all sorts of questions about where the City was. He had a pith helmet and baggy trousers to his knees.'

Desdemona flapped her wings apprehensively.

'A pith helmet?' rumbled Bone, the beads of sweat building on his brow. 'What sort of pith helmet?'

'Well,' Mendoza said, concentrating, 'it was sort of. . .sort of——'

'It was a *jaunty* pith helmet,' said Dolores. 'So what?'

From his most plecaritudinous depths,* Captain Neptune Bone started to rumble. It began with a tremor beneath his belly, then it spread to an out-of-control vibration in his chest, rising through his throat until it hit his vocal chords with a tempestuous fury.

---

* The place from where human venom springs.

'*Cairo Jim!*' he exploded.

'Craaaaaaark!' screamed Desdemona, springing from his shoulder and landing on Mendoza's hair.

'You...you know of him, Senor von Mostetot?' asked Dolores, puzzled.

Bone certainly *did* know of him. Some time previously they had worked together on a dig at the Bent Pyramid at Saqqara. They had fallen out over a certain Flight Attendant who had come to assist them as a volunteer, and now the bearded man despised this Cairo Jim. The jaunty pith helmet wearer was always on time when paying his annual membership fees to the Old Relics Society, and he was a goody-goody to boot.

But Bone remembered his deception and clenched his teeth grindingly.

'Yes,' he seethed, 'I *have* heard of him. I read about him in a story in *Picturegoer* magazine. Arrrrr. Apparently he's well-known.'

'He was a gentleman,' sighed Dolores. 'And so I told him where to begin looking for the City.'

'You did *what*?'

'Wouldn't it be funny, senor,' Mendoza chuckled, 'if he were to be there when we arrived? You could put him in your picture, perhaps. He would make a fine movie star.'

'He had such a charming smile,' said Dolores.

By now, Bone was white with rage. 'I'll put him in the picture, all right! Yupichu!' he howled through the megaphone. 'Take us to the City as quickly as you can! Take any shortcut you know! We will travel through the night without sleeping, we will have our meals as we go, we will not stop for a single thing, not even a manicure. *We must move like lightning's fury!*'

He lowered the megaphone and his temples throbbed loudly. 'Fortune itself depends on it,' he rumbled menacingly into his beard.

12

ARRIVAL

IT was evening, early enough for the last glimmers of daylight to be dancing on the horizon, yet late enough for the moon to be suspended high in the pale twilight sky.

There was a full moon this evening—perfectly round, brilliantly white, glowingly soft around the edges. Strong beams emanated from it in all directions, and far below, the mountaintop of HokeyCokey was bathed in the wash of its celestial coolness and the dying embers of the day.

As Doris and Cairo Jim stood before the Moongate, they both felt a strange thrill in the air. Without a word they fluttered and ducked under the low-hanging rock arch, and flew and stepped through the arch itself.

There above them, at the end of a narrow path which skittered up and away, lay an unparalleled view. Jim gasped, and a full symphony orchestra began playing beneath his breastbone.

'The Lost City of the Dancers,' he whispered.

'The very place itself,' Doris crooned.

He raised his binoculars. Slowly he moved his magnified gaze from one end of the City to the other.

It was not what he had expected, and Doris was right: it looked nothing like the engraving in the book. There were no castellated battlements riding the crest of the mountaintop, no towers or buttresses like spikes on the back of a dinosaur. Instead he found himself looking up at a small exposed area on the pinnacle of the mountain, where a steep outcrop had been neatly terraced with forty or fifty simple, squarish, flat-topped rooms of rock. Each room appeared to have one window hole and one door hole.

'Gosh,' he said quietly. 'How beautiful. How simple and beautiful.'

Rising all around the square dwellings was a network of high paths and steps which connected each room to the next. Many of the steps at the top of the City were green with moss and thick with small bushes, and some were completely camouflaged by the overgrowth. He immediately thought how steep they would be to climb, and how dangerous it would be if he were to fall.

Moving the binoculars down, he came across a big, round courtyard in the centre of the outcrop. That, he assumed, was one of the dancing arenas Doris had mentioned in her story. The rock which made up the floor of this courtyard looked much smoother than the surrounding walls, and already the moonlight was reflecting milkily off it.

He now raised his binoculars to the very top of ChaCha Muchos. A large, tumbly-looking tower protruded from the mountain. Its walls were circular and it looked as if at one stage there had been a conical roof, for he could spy several large beams of heavy wood rising to a point amidst the trees which had grown up through the centre of the tower.

'That's odd,' he said.

'Raark.' Doris was perched on the low rock wall at the edge of the Moongate. 'What's odd?'

'That tower. It seems to be the only building in the whole City that's grown over. Apart from the steps and the tower, everywhere else appears as if it's been looked after, as though the jungle and the weeds and the dirt have all been cleared away.'

'The Indians,' Doris flapped. 'They do it every year whenever they come up. It's a ritual with them.'

'I wonder why they neglect the tower,' mused Jim. He turned his binoculars to the left, then to the right, then slowly down. It appeared that there was a point, an imaginary line, above the flat stone roofs of the upper dwellings. Below this line the City was neat and tidy, but above it everything verged on jungle. And the tower was the thickest, tangliest bit of all.

'I don't know,' Doris said. 'It's been the same ever since I've been following them here. They never go near it.'

As Jim continued eyeing the tower, something began to appear. Slowly, silently, wispishly, like spectral fingers materialising out of nowhere, a grey fog was forming. The fingers seeped through the windows and door holes, and clutched around the corners of the dwellings. Soon the tower and some of the uppermost rooms were invisible.

'Raark,' Doris raarked, watching it and blinking. 'We'd better hit the trail. There may be enough moonlight to see the path now, but if that fog gets any thicker we'll be as blind as bats in a——'

'Doris,' interrupted Jim, spying something else.

'What?'

'Fog doesn't usually rise in thin columns, does it?'

She shook her head. 'Not any I've seen.'

'Take a look at this.' He held the binoculars out and the mighty bird came and flapped onto his shoulder for the first time. She squinted and put her open eye against the eyepiece. 'Reerark! That's not fog, that's smoke.'

Jim looked at her.

'Probably the Indians,' she said. 'They're usually there by now. Lower these spyglasses a fraction.'

He did so.

'Si,' she rerked. 'I see where it's coming from. Over there to the right, in the bush next to the City.'

Jim took back the binoculars and looked again.

'They always make their camp in the bush. They only go into the City in the daytime, to clean it and then to sit and wait.'

'So if we arrive tonight we won't disturb them?'

'Hopefully not,' answered the macaw.

'Are they hostile, these Indians?'

Doris thought for a moment. 'They are *wary*,' she said. 'They, too, have seen what humans from the other world are capable of.' She hopped off his shoulder and flitted before him. 'Come,' she cooed. 'It is time we were moving. This night will be a fitting cloak.'

Jim put the binoculars away and fastened down his

knapsack. Then, their movements wrapped in silence, they began to climb the final section of the trail to ChaCha Muchos.

It was well and truly dark by the time Cairo Jim and Doris arrived at the end of the paved trail. The last bit of the journey had taken precisely two hours and three minutes (they stopped only once, when Jim had to prise some small, furry berries from the sole of his boot). The fog was now thick and soupy.

They stood panting before two huge piles of rock, which long ago would have held a gate. Even Doris was out of breath.

'The entrance to the City,' she prowked.

'At last,' puffed Cairo Jim.

A soft chorus of chatter and singing came from the direction of the Indians' fire, wafting across on the vapour of fog and the tremor of moonlight.

'They seem happy tonight,' observed the macaw.

'Maybe their Sandra is coming tomorrow,' smiled Jim. He took a swig from his water bottle and wiped his forehead under the brim of his pith helmet. Then he took out his torch. 'Come on,' he whispered. 'Let's make *our* camp.'

'Where?'

'How about that tower up there? It'll be good protection from the wind and it seems the ideal place if, as you say, the Indians don't go near it.'

She hesitated and her feathers ruffled.

'What's wrong?' asked Jim. 'You're not *afraid*, are you?'

'Scraark,' she flustered indignantly. 'Of course I'm not afraid. It's just . . .'

'Yes?'

'Methinks there's something funny about that place. Look at it. There's something *foreboding* up there.'

He looked up at the silent, brooding structure, just visible beneath the swirling fog. At this close distance it seemed to be almost on top of them. Elsewhere the moonlight was shining off the walls of the dwellings in a dull, whitish glow, but here the glow was altogether different: much greener and, it seemed to his weary eyes, *pulsating*. It was as though the tumbly edifice had a rhythm all its own—a silent, heart-beating rhythm.

Cairo Jim took a deep breath and blinked. 'We're just tired, that's all.' He switched on the torch, being careful to keep its beam on the ground directly in front of his feet. 'Come on, I'll need you to keep an eye on me up these stairs. I don't want to break my neck after coming this far.'

Doris gulped. 'Rightio,' she squawked, 'but I still feel funny about sleeping up there.'

From some unknown, hidden reservoir deep inside himself, Jim found a last burst of energy and, with Doris circling above his pith helmet, he bounded all the way to the top of the nearly vertical staircase, not thinking once about its perilous steepness.

At the top he caught his breath. Doris came and perched on his shoulder and together they viewed the City sloping away below them. The moon glinted in the puddles of rainwater lying about, and the whole place was majestic and still.

History hung all about them.

'How sad,' breathed Jim, in awe of it all.

'Reerk,' reerked Doris.

He turned to the tower. It was hard to recognise it as the mysterious structure they had seen from the Moongate. Vines and leaves sprouted from cracks in its walls, and it seemed to be crawling with rustling undergrowth. Slowly he cast his torchbeam across it. 'Can you see a door, my dear?' he whispered.

'Keep shining,' she cooed. She was uneasy about the idea of going inside, but somehow Cairo Jim was comforting. 'Wait! There. That dark hole.'

'Come on then.'

He took his machete and, crouching, made his way through the confusion of leaves and fronds. 'You're right, Doris. It's a little doorway. Stay close.'

'I'm not going anywhere you're not.'

Together they ducked into the rambling, foreboding tower.

The next thing Jim heard was an ear-splitting *'Screee-aaaarrrk!'*

He opened his eyes and sat bolt upright. The morning light was streaming down through roof beams and leaves. He blinked a couple of times and looked around before he remembered where he was.

'Screeeaaaarrrk!' came the noise again.

Above him, Doris was parading along a branch. 'Welcome to the land of the living.'

'Thank you,' said Jim. 'I slept like a log.'

'You slumbered crashingly last night,' she said, opening her wings and folding them about her. 'No sooner had you thrown down your blanket than you were on it and snoring loudly like an earthquake.'

'I must have been exhausted.'

'So I took your torch and had an explore. It's just an old tower with some weeds and trees and things, nothing more. I don't know why you were so scared.' She hopped up and down in a superior kind of way.

Jim stood and began inspecting their surroundings. The interior was about six paces in diameter. There were no windows, unlike the other dwellings, and the door hole was barely big enough for a grown person to fit through. In the centre a huge tree rose from the earth floor, its uppermost branches mingling with a few heavy beams of rotting wood. To one side of the tree, on the ground, was a large mound of ivy-covered earth. Jim sat on this and looked up at the walls.

They were solid rock and the surface was very uneven, with small alcoves of different depths spaced irregularly along. Some of these alcoves were quite deep, and could have served as shelves or hiding-holes for small objects, while others were shallow and more like blemishes in the texture of the rock. Great clumps of moss grew here and there, and in those spaces where there was no moss, Jim could see marks on the rock, as though something had been smeared across. He looked at these marks carefully, then took his journal and a pencil from his knapsack and jotted something down.

Doris was hopping up and down on the ground by the door hole. 'Jim! Jim! Look at this!' she screeched.

The archaeologist–poet closed his journal and went and crouched next to her.

Fixed horizontally above the door was a long piece of coarse rope. All the way along it were large knots in different shapes and sizes, sometimes two or three together, sometimes only one by itself. In some of the knots a condor's feather had been inserted, and in others, pieces of faded fabric in long, plaited strips were interwoven.

'What is it?' asked Jim.

'A message,' prowked Doris. 'From the ChaCha Muchonians.'

'What does it say?'

The bird turned to him. 'Luckily I can read ancient ChaCha Muchonian knot language,' she announced. 'It is an identification message, commonly used to mark territory in ancient times.'

'Whose territory?'

She turned to the rope. 'Let's see. . .' Clearing her throat, she began to read: *'Here stands the dwelling place of Sandra daughter of Sancho leader of ChaCha Muchonians and maker of Clackersmackers a wise and rhythmical woman chachacha.'*

'Doris!' whispered Jim excitedly. 'We're in Sandra Panza's tower! These very walls housed perhaps the most important person in all the City!' He sighed. 'If only they could speak, if only they could tell us what happened to Sandra, why she plummeted from the battlements the way she did, what became of the people after she had gone.' He stroked his chin. 'Does it say anything else?'

'Nope, that's it.'

'Hmm. And there doesn't seem to be anything else in here that holds any message. We'll have to search the City.' He stood and went to the centre of the tower, his hands clasped behind his back. 'Doris,' he said in his best archaeological tone, 'here is what I propose we do: because this place seems to be out of bounds to the Indians, who may be a disturbance to us in our work, it will make the perfect base. We can store our things here during the day while we inspect the dwellings below. Then at night we can gather some food from the jungle and return here to eat and read, and write up our day's findings. We'll continue to do so until we've found what we're after. Sound good?'

'Raark,' she nodded.

'Fine.' He started emptying his knapsack of the things they would not need. When his framed photo of Jocelyn Osgood fell out he propped it up on top of the ivy-covered mound. 'What time do the Indians come into the City each morning?'

The macaw peered up at the sky through the branches and leaves. 'Soon,' she answered. 'Very soon. They will go and clean the lower dwellings and then sit in the huge dancing arena, sometimes dancing, but all the time waiting. Then, when the sun goes down, they will go back to the bush.'

'Right,' he said, putting on his pith helmet and hoisting his now lighter knapsack over his shoulders. 'Then let's go down now. It'd be good if they didn't to see us during our visit. We don't want to interfere with their ritual.'

'You have great respect,' Doris prerked.

'Come on, my dear,' he said, extending his arm.

For the rest of the day they explored as many dwellings as they could without drawing the Indians' attention to themselves. This involved a good deal of scampering from one dwelling to another, usually up and down the almost perpendicular staircases, trying to be as quiet as butterflies.

The rooms on the whole were much the same inside as out—simple, small enclosures, all of them with dirt floors packed hard by time, all of them empty and free from ornaments or decoration. Jim and Doris found no more knotted lengths of string hanging anywhere.

Late in the afternoon, while they were in the twentieth house, Doris turned to him. 'Maybe,' she said, 'they buried things beneath the floor? Why don't you have a dig?'

He smiled and took out his pocket knife. With the sharp thing ideal for getting small furry berries out of the soles of his boots, he started to break up the hard dirt floor.

Suddenly there was a loud *snap*, and the sharp thing broke asunder.

'Reeerk!' screeched Doris, diving out of the way as half of it flew across the room.

'Goodness,' said Jim. He put down the knife and scratched the dirt away with his fingers. 'Look, Doris. It's all rock underneath.'

'Coo,' she cooed, waddling closer.

'The same rock as the walls.' He scratched away some more earth from the floor. 'Look here. See those marks? That look like smears?'

'Raark, just like the walls.'

'Exactly like the walls. It was the same in the tower; I made a drawing of them in my journal. And look, see how the floor and the walls here also have these little uneven holes all over the place?'

'Si, I see.'

'Remember what the legend says about the potion? How the Indians built the City by carving out the very rock face with this formula? This must be how they did it.'

'Rerk. I don't understand.'

He stood and rubbed his hands over the wall. 'Tell me once again—what couldn't the potion dissolve?'

'Leather,' squawked the macaw. 'It could eat into everything except leather.'

'So maybe they took some hides of leather and poured some of the potion onto them and then rubbed them against the rock, round and round, until they'd hollowed out enough of a space to crawl into. Then they poured more potion on the hides, and rubbed some more, and gradually enough rock was worn away to make a room. That would account for all those smeary marks!'

'What about the uneven alcoves?' Doris flapped.

'Perhaps they were formed whenever fresh potion was poured onto the leather. When they put this fresh, stronger potion straight onto the rock it dissolved the surface very quickly. The older the potion got, the weaker it became and the less it dissolved, so then it made only small holes.'

'And the door and window holes—easy! They just poured the potion directly onto the rock until it ate all the way through. Raaaaark!' she flapped, hopping up and down.

'I should never have doubted it when I read it in the book,' he sighed, sliding down the wall and sitting on the floor. He frowned and rubbed his chin.

'What's wrong, Jim?'

'It still doesn't solve my problem,' he said. 'It's all very fascinating to know how they built the place, but I need to know what *happened* to them. Where did they go? *That's* the knowledge worth getting. Why, without it, my whole trip——'

At that point both he and Doris nearly jumped out of their skins at the colossal commotion which burst forth boomingly from below.

13

CHACHACHICANERY

'SHE comes?' shouted the Indians again, their voices as loud as an ocean wave.

'Si,' nodded Yupichu impatiently. 'Listen, you can hear Her music! She brings it with Her, as the legend said She would!'

A current of excitement swelled through the tribe. Zapateado stepped before them and raised his smooth hand. 'Hush, my people,' he commanded. 'Let us listen.'

The crowd fell silent, and they heard a distant, high-pitched screeching. The noise came closer. Many of the Indians put their hands over their ears, unsure as to whether it was the worst sound they had heard, but there was no mistaking it—it was music!

Yupichu thumped his chest with his closed fist. '*I* have brought Her,' he boasted. '*I* have returned Our Sandra to Her people!'

Suddenly an enormous bundle of boxes, canvas and travelling trunks scuttled into the arena. The Indians gasped and moved back a few steps. The paraphernalia was quickly dumped unceremoniously on the ground, and there emerged a stocky man with the strangest hair the Indians had ever seen. Some of the younger, wizened children giggled and were shushed by their mothers. Mendoza looked curiously at the gathering, then went to wait in a corner by the stairs.

Now something truly startling entered. Sweating up the staircase, huffing and puffing heavily, came a huge, prune-smelling, hairy-faced being with a great smoking column hanging from its mouth. On its head it wore a squat, mulberry-coloured cylinder with a short black tassel. The being had an emerald-green torso-covering, with a big gold chain attached to the front which disappeared into a slit. Under all this was another covering of Alsatian-dog hue. Its legs were covered by baggy, checked cloth, gathered just below its pudgy kneecaps; it had floral stockings on its calves; and its feet had black and white patches all over them.

This strange, dragon-type thing climbed up onto the largest travelling trunk and blew smoke all around. It wheezed heavily and raised a long, metallic cone to its flabby mouth. By now the music was very loud. The being waved a manicured hand over the crowd (many of the Indian women admired the neat, polished fingernails) and, as a huge black bird with throbbing red eyes came to rest on the front of the trunk, the music abruptly stopped.

'See,' Yupichu whispered to Zapateado, 'this is Her Guardian.'

'Shh,' said Zapateado, 'it is about to speak.'

A shaft of smoke shot out of the end of the megaphone and Neptune Bone began booming. 'Good evening, ladies and gentlemen and everyone else. This is indeed a great, monumental occasion for you all, for today, after hundreds of interminable years, your waiting is at an end!'

Some of the older Indians nodded and whispered and shuffled their feet.

'It has been a long journey all the way from the Empire of Clouds, but today I, Otto of the Heavens, am proud to present your Awaited: your All-Seeing, All-Knowing, All-Dancing *Sandra the Celestial*!'

A low, intense murmur of expectation went up and down the tribe, and their eyes glittered with hope.

Seconds passed, agonisingly long seconds, each of them seeming longer than all the time the Indians and their ancestors had been waiting.

But nothing happened.

Bone looked displeased and removed the megaphone from his mouth. 'Madam!' he hissed through clenched teeth, 'that was your cue!'

'Keep your poncho on,' came an irritated voice. Then up the giant staircase, step by step, her back ramrod straight, marched Dolores del Tempo. She had never appeared taller in all her life.

'Oh, dear,' muttered Mendoza.

The red-frilled woman stood before them in her most astonishing stilettos, her violin and bow clutched by her sides, a black lacy handkerchief veiling her face. She was as imposing as the mountaintop itself.

Every Indian present sucked in their breath, including Zapateado. The old man reached out a trembling arm. 'Oh, what a great height! Welcome, Our Long Awaited,' he croaked, his voice catching in his throat. 'Welcome back to Your City.'

A small tear he had been storing all his life escaped

out of the corner of his eye and rolled haltingly down his cheek, and he sank slowly to his knees. His tribespeople uttered something together from a lost language and followed his example.

'Look, Mendoza,' Dolores whispered, 'look at their faces. See how the old ones look young, and the young ones look old? I bet I am right!'

'I hope so,' said Mendoza quietly, his stomach feeling strange.

Bone smirked at the kneeling mass and put the megaphone to his lips once again. 'My friends,' he bellowed, 'it has been an exhausting trip for Us all. Not only did I, Otto of the Heavens, have to protect Madam...ahem, Our Sandra...from the wilds of the jungle, but I also had to be on the lookout for white-hatted demons who wanted to stop Her from appearing before you today.' He looked around snarlingly.

'What is he talking about, "white-hatted demons"?' whispered Dolores.

'Search me,' shrugged Mendoza.

'And so, for My troubles,' Bone continued, 'you must reward Me accordingly.'

'What?' Dolores hissed.

'Then I will leave Our Sandra with you and return to the Heavens once more.'

'What?' she hissed again.

Zapateado raised his head. 'What would You like, Otto of the Heavens? Would you like us to prepare a feast? We could kill a boar and——'

'Ha!' came the ringing, metallic laugh. 'We celestial beings do not eat. We are Divine!'

'Then what is it you desire?'

Captain Neptune Flannelbottom Bone puffed out his chest and pushed back his shoulders. This was his moment of triumph. 'I desire,' he purred, 'the most valuable thing in the possession of this tribe. That is all. No more, no less.'

Zapateado grimaced as he thought what this could be. *The most valuable thing.* He shook his head sadly.

'I am sorry,' he said, taking the small leather pouch from his belt and holding it tightly, 'but all we have of any value is what is here in this pouch. It has been passed down from generation to generation and is the last of its kind. The knowledge of its making disappeared many centuries ago, with the untimely death of its maker. I am afraid I cannot let it go. There is great responsibility attached to this. . .you see, it is our whole heritage.'

'Arrr,' wobbled Bone excitedly. 'What, pray tell, is in the pouch?'

Zapateado spoke as softly as a feather falling. 'The very essence of this City, the last remaining sample of the potion which built these walls.'

'Thank *you*,' shouted Bone. 'At it, Desdemona!'

'Wait a minuto,' shouted Dolores, 'that's *mine*!'

She lunged out to take the pouch, but was not quick enough; in less than an instant, the flea-ridden raven had plucked the leather sack from the old man's grasp and had delivered it to the clammy palm of Bone.

His eyes filled with the greatest delight. 'At last, at last, my fortune is at hand,' he gloated ecstatically.

'Craaark! Now I want them toes,' the raven drooled.

'*Hold it right there, you underhanded usurper!*' came a voice from high above.

The Indians gasped and turned to see Cairo Jim standing defiantly atop the staircase leading to the tower, peering through his binoculars. Doris perched upon his pith helmet, her feathers bristling.

'Arrrr,' Bone arrrred. It *was* a jaunty pith helmet.

'Look, senorita,' said Mendoza, 'it is Cairo Jim!'

'So it is,' said Dolores del Tempo. 'Maybe he will get my potion back.'

'My good people,' Bone rumbled, thinking quickly. 'See! There upon that stair is one of the white-hatted demons of whom I spoke. He will stop at nothing to keep Our Sandra from you. He must be destroyed immediately!'

The large man leapt from the travelling trunk and, flinging open the lid, heaved out the antique Ottoman Empire miniature cannon with cannonball inside. Resting the muzzle on the head of Desdemona, he aimed the weapon straight at Jim and Doris. 'This'll make you whistle, Cairo Jim,' he sniggered fiendishly.

'It's no use, Neptune Bone,' cried Jim. 'That thing has about as much firing power as you do.'

'Who is "Neptune Bone"?' said Mendoza, scratching his hair (which had become quite lopsided). He looked up towards the archaeologist–poet. 'Hola, Senor Cairo, what do you mean? This is Senor Otto von Mostetot, the famous film director.'

'If that's von Mostetot I'm the Colossus of Rhodes. No, Mendoza, I'm afraid that is Neptune Bone, the most notorious archaeologist in the history of the Old Relics Society! And the most unfinancial!'

'What?' Mendoza started to shake. He glared at Bone. 'You...you *deceived* us?'

'So what if I did?' snarled Bone. 'You won't live to tell another soul, Cairo Jim. It's tomb-time for you!' He turned to Yupichu. 'Got a match, Yupichu? Arr, never mind, I'll use this.'

He flicked open his silver cigar-lighter and held the flint near the cannon's fuse.

'Bye, bye, you white-hatted demon,' he growled.

And, with a fierce burst of laughter, he lowered the flame to the fuse.

14

A TRAGIC LOSS

'You deceiver!' shouted Mendoza, rushing towards the cannon.

'No, Mendoza!' cried Dolores del Tempo, 'you'll be blasted!'

But Mendoza could not hear her; his rage was bubbling like boiling water up into his ears. 'Deceiver!' he shouted again, his eyes wild and fearsome.

'Now, just a minute, little man,' said Bone, watching the fuse sizzle quickly down. 'Move away or you'll find yourself ventilated in a place you'd rather not.'

'You deceive these good people with your stupido charade, and now I find you have deceived Miss del Tempo all this time!'

'Time?' snapped Bone, a bead of perspiration dripping from under his fez. 'Time? That is a commodity of which you do not have a lot right at this moment.'

'Mendoza!' shrieked Dolores. 'Move away! You'll perish in the nastiest manner!'

The fuse crackled and hissed, burning quicker and quicker, closer and closer to the cannon. *Szszszszszs.*

'*Craaaark!*' screamed Desdemona, her head pinioned. 'Move away or we'll *all* go up!'

'NO!' shouted the brave Mendoza, crossing his arms and positioning himself directly in front of the weapon's bore. 'Not until this *scoundrel* gives me that pouch for Miss del Tempo.'

'Not on your Nellie,' Bone growled.

'Mendoza!' Dolores shrieked again, growing faint. She steadied herself against a kneeling Indian named Charleston, who immediately felt honoured.

szszszszszszszszs crackled the fuse, louder by the second.

'Hand it back to its rightful owners, Bone,' hollered Cairo Jim, 'or by Nespernub I'll make sure you pay.'

'Nevermore!' squawked Desdemona.

'Mendoza, my dear, protective amigo,' gasped Dolores, 'do not bother! Your life is more important than a stupid pouch——'

The noble Mendoza turned his head to her and took a long look. Then he smiled. 'No, senorita of my dreams, your happiness is——'

szszszszszszszszszszszszszszszszszszszs!
'Move away, Wonky!'
'Never, you scoundrel!'
'Hand it back, Bone!'
'Reeerrraaaarrrk!'
'Arrk, I've got a flea in my——'
'Mendoza, my dear——'

POOOOH!

The ancient cannon spewed its missile with the same amount of force as a one-hundred-year-old spider. The dusty cannonball rolled slowly out of the cannon and plopped against the belly of a disbelieving Mendoza, who caught it in his arms. At the same time, the cannon began to roll back off Desdemona's head, pushing itself against the bulk of Neptune Bone.

'What the——?' he puffed, trying to stop the weight, but it was heavier than he had thought. He stepped backwards, and backwards again, his right hand still clutching the precious pouch, but the weapon would not stop; back and back it rolled, and Bone could not get out of its path. He was being steamrolled towards the edge of the dancing arena, to a spot where the battlement walls had long ago been worn away and had crumbled and fallen thousands of metres into the raging Marjangower River.

He huffed and puffed, he grunted and gasped, all the while trying to grind the archaic weapon to a halt, but it had a mind of its own. The farther it rolled, the faster it became. The Indians watched in horrified silence.

Then, just as Neptune Bone lurched backwards onto the very edge of the dancing arena, onto the very last centimetre where he could safely stand, the cannon stopped with a rusty squeak.

'Ha!' Bone snorted. 'So much for karma. Come Desdemona, let's vamoose.' He turned on his heel. 'Those doors——*aaaaaaaarrrrrrrrrggggggggghhhhhhhh!*'

The ornate, manicured, pruneponging man was plummeting into the abyss, turning cartwheels in the air, getting smaller by the second. His fez blew off and, in the worst moment of his life to date, the potion went hurtling from him, spilling all the way down into the blasting Marjangower.

'Champion!' cried Cairo Jim.

'Creeerraarrk!' screamed Desdemona. 'I'm off! Nevermoooooore. . .' And she whooooshed off like a tatty missile into the safety of the skies.

The Indians rushed to the edge of the arena and looked over, where they beheld a terrible sight. With a near-deafening *sluuuuuurp*, the great river was evaporating before their very eyes, disappearing into nothing itself! Away and away it *sluuuuuuuurp*ed, the water swirling like a hellish whirlpool. The noise was like a thousand drowning men.

When the water had gurgled to a stop, all that remained was a scattering of boulders in a bone-dry riverbed.

Bone-dry was right. The crazed Captain was nowhere to be seen. (Only Jim and Doris, standing much higher on the stairs, glimpsed his fattish figure inching its way along a leafy branch far, far below.)

Dolores del Tempo threw off her veil and rushed to Mendoza. 'My amigo!' she cried, lifting him by the shoulders and planting a heavily lipsticked kiss on his forehead. 'You were prepared to perish for me. What a magnificent soul!' She lowered him gently to the ground.

Mendoza straightened his spine and Dolores could not help gasping with astonishment. Somehow he looked different; there was some kind of new aura about him. For the first time, he appeared to be on her level.

'Miss del Tempo,' he declared. 'The time has come

for a revelation. All this time people have thought Mendoza a clumsy but gentle fool. ''Not good with things as a rule,'' I have heard it often said. But Love has many disguises.' He blushed quickly. 'Miss del Tempo, I have a confession.'

'Yes?' said Dolores, her eyes brimming with the shining sight of him.

Mendoza spoke gravely. 'I have been deceiving you all this time.'

'What?' Her lip trembled.

'Si. You see, I am not really Mendoza, the obliging helping-hand at the Popocatepetl Club. No. I am——' and he whipped off his wonky wig to reveal his handsome, baby-bottom smooth bald head, 'Mendoza, Lord of the Eastern Andes and last of the Inca Princes!'

'Well, jiggle me on a stick and call me a maraca!' gasped Dolores.

'But you may call me Maurice,' he said.

'And you, my *darling*, may call me *Dolores* del Tempo.'

'Will you become my Princess, Dolores del Tempo?' asked the Prince.

Dolores opened her mouth to answer, but at that moment there was a mighty collective roar from the Indians.

'Come on!' said Mendoza, grabbing her by the hand. 'Let's vamoose.'

Zapateado was standing before the tribe, shaking with rage and confusion. 'My people,' he shouted angrily, 'we have lost all that is ours, all that has ever been ours. Now we will always grow old like the rest of the world...'

'No! No! No!' bellowed the crowd.

There was a clatter of hoofs, and up from below came the huge camel, snorting wildly as she sensed the impending danger. She stopped before the throng and raised her eyes to the top of the staircase. And her heart (and eyelashes) fluttered!

Cairo Jim lost his balance for a second, dizzy at the sight of her. He swayed, then stood firm. 'Brenda!' he shouted. 'Doris, it's Brenda, all the way from the Valley of the Kings. I'd know her snort anywhere!'

Brenda the Wonder Camel snorted again and galloped through the scattering crowd and up the stairs to Cairo Jim and Doris. Jim gave her a snoutingly good rub and introduced her to the macaw.

Zapateado pointed at the trio. 'And they are responsible!' he shouted wrathfully. 'The white-hatted demon and his animals have spilled our potion! They have taken our heritage!'

The crowd growled, incited by the rage of their leader.

'I don't like the look of this,' screeched Doris.

'Capture them! Advance and capture the demons! The fire ants will have their hides!'

The crowd surged forwards, jostling, pushing, shoving. They spilled up the stairs like a spreading shadow.

'Come on, gang!' yelled Cairo Jim. 'Into the tower!'

Suddenly there was a common gasp from the Indians. Together, as though they were one person, they all sank to their knees wherever they were. Every eye was staring, wide with amazement, into the sky behind Jim, Doris and Brenda.

Jim turned to face where they were looking, and he too gasped.

For high above, the great curtain of the sky had been pulled apart and an enormous ball of bright, bright orange was rising slowly behind the tower.

And a huge burst of strange music filled the air.

15

THE SECOND COMING

'SHE comes!' cried Zapateado, his arms outstretched towards the orb of orange. 'Our Sandra comes!'

It rose slowly, becoming bigger and bigger until it seemed to fill the entire sky above the City. As it did so, the music swelled louder and louder.

'She brings Her music!' Zapateado shouted. 'From Her great height She brings Her music! We have been wrong, my people. That——' and he pointed to Dolores, already becoming a distant sight, 'is not Sandra of the Heavens. No, we have been led a merry dance! Behold, there She comes on high!'

'Well I'll be swoggled,' muttered Cairo Jim.

The ball rose and expanded, and then something odd appeared. Emerging from behind the rotting timbers of the tower roof came a pattern of ropes. Under those came a huge wicker basket filled with small men in natty green hats with feathers. All of these men were playing musical instruments and having a jolly time. At the front of the basket, standing alone, was a figure wearing dark goggles and a leather helmet with curved horns on top.

'I don't believe it,' said Jim, smiling.

'Hullo, Jim!' hollered Jocelyn Osgood. 'I hope I haven't come at a bad time, I just thought I'd—wooooops!'

A quick gust of wind caught the basket and sent it crashing into the tree and the timbers of the tower roof, where it became wedged tight. The balloon billowed helplessly above it.

'Yaargh!' shouted Terry's Tyroleans, falling about and dropping their instruments.

Zapateado looked up and addressed his kneeling tribe. 'Behold, She has entered Her tower! She has returned to Her Place of Being. Let us wait for Her to appear before us!'

'Quick,' Jim said to Doris and Brenda, 'inside!'

'Reeeraark!'

'Quaaaooo!'

They rushed up the last few steps and ducked in to find Jocelyn climbing expertly down the grizzled tree.

'So,' she said, unstrapping her helmet and shaking out her curly hair, 'this is ChaCha Muchos?'

'Yes,' said Jim. 'Am I glad to see you!'

'How sweet,' said Jocelyn. 'Brenda! Fancy you being here!'

'Quaaao!' snorted the Bactrian.

'Oh, what a beautiful parrot!'

'Raaaaaaark!' screeched Doris.

'She's a macaw,' corrected Jim quickly. 'Doris, I'd like you to meet Miss Osgood.'

'Good evening,' blinked the bird.

'Hullo.' Jocelyn shook Doris's claw, then looked up at the inhabitants of the basket. 'Be still up there, you fellows! If you break that basket we'll *really* be in hot water.'

There was a huge, wishful sigh from above.

'What are they doing here?' Jim asked.

Jocelyn rolled her eyes. 'They weren't *invited*. I hired the balloon—thought I'd surprise you after what you said about those lines at Nazca—and I was just about to cast off when they all appeared out of nowhere and piled into the basket without asking. I couldn't get them out. Seems they'd been following me. A girl can't go anywhere these days without being hounded.'

'It must have been very crowded.'

'No, not really. Luckily we picked up a good wind and made it here in record time.' She placed her hands on her hips and peered out through the door hole. 'Now, what's all this about "Our Sandra" and "Sandra of the Heavens"'?'

Together Jim and Doris explained the whole story. When they had finished, Jocelyn laughed out loud.

'Dolores? Celestial? Ha, ha. I'm glad about Mendoza, though. They're probably heading back, if I know her. And Bone? What of him?'

'We saw him shinning along a bough of a giant fern he must have grabbed on the way down. He looked like he was trembling a good deal, and he was very white.'

'That's the last we'll see of him, I hope.'

Jim sighed. 'So that only leaves us.'

Jocelyn leaned against the wall and ran a hand through her disordered locks. 'You sound glum, Jim,' she said.

'Oh, I shouldn't be, should I? After all, Brenda and I have been reunited——'

'Quaaooo.'

'——and I've made a new friend, a noble new friend.'

Doris blushed and spread her wings.

'And we *have* found the City. . .'

'But something's wrong, isn't it?' asked Jocelyn.

Jim sat down on the ivy-covered mound, his boot knocking against it with a faint clang. 'I still haven't found the reason for the disappearance of the ChaCha Muchonians.'

Brenda lumbered around behind him and started sniffing close to the ground while Doris waddled after her.

'It would help if we knew what we were looking for,' Jim sighed.

Brenda scraped a hoof in the dirt behind the mound.

'We've looked just about everywhere,' said Jim. 'Most of the dwellings down there are——'

'Quaaaaaoooo!'

'——are——'

'Quaaaaaoooo!'

'I think Brenda's trying to tell you something,' Jocelyn said.

Jim turned to her. 'What is it, my lovely?'

She fluttered her eyelashes and knocked against the ivy with her hoof. It clanged and echoed loudly.

'Rark,' squawked Doris, 'she's found something underneath!'

Jim sprang off the mound and crouched down

before it. He gave it a sharp rap with his knuckles. *Clang* it went again.

'So she has.' He took out his pocket knife and quickly scraped off a small patch of ivy and dirt. It fell away to reveal an area the colour of dull silver. 'It looks like some sort of pot,' said Jim.

'It's very large for a pot,' said Jocelyn.

'Maybe it's a cauldron?' suggested Doris. 'Like the witches used in Senor Shakespeare's Scottish play.'

Jim looked up, his eyes blazing with excitement. 'Of course! Of course! Doris, you clever bird. And Brenda, you Wonderful set of humps. Do you know what we have here?'

They all looked at him, waiting for the answer.

'If I'm not mistaken, this will be the pot...the cauldron...which Sandra Panza used to cook up her Clackersmackers!'

Doris hopped up and down, her tail feathers tingling.

'Let's turn it over,' said Jocelyn.

'Right,' nodded Jim. He and Jocelyn scraped away more ivy and dirt, and Jim ran the blade of the knife around where the lip of the vessel rested on the floor. Doris removed the photograph of Jocelyn from the top of the mound and deposited it in a corner. Then Jim and Jocelyn prised their fingers under the lip and, with a straining grunt, they turned the huge cauldron onto its side.

'Phew,' puffed Jocelyn.

Doris waddled into the centre of it. 'Smells like it's made of lead,' she cooed. 'Raark! Here's something!'

'What is it, Doris? Bring it here.'

The macaw dragged out a long rope tied full of knots and condor feathers and pieces of fabric and small animal bones. It was in much better condition than the identification message suspended above the door, because it had been locked in the airtight chamber of the cauldron, completely undisturbed.

'Ancient ChaCha Muchonian knot language,' Jim told Jocelyn.

'What does it say?'

'Can you read it, Doris?'

The bird nodded. 'It appears to be a recipe,' she squawked.

'A recipe?'

'For something sweet, by the look of things.'

Jim thumped his fist into his palm. 'Clacker-smackers!' he cried. 'I'll bet you a pyramid it's for Clackersmackers. Why else would it be in there? Can you decipher it, my dear?'

She blinked and her beak creased around the edges. 'Of course I can. But first,' she lowered her voice, 'you must make me a promise.'

'Anything,' said Cairo Jim. 'Anything that I can do, I promise you I will.'

'When you leave this place, you must take me and Senor Shakespeare back to Egypt with you.'

'Is that all?' laughed the archaeologist. 'My dear, dear Doris, I had planned to ask you anyway. I can't imagine going back without you. Why,' he reached over and tousled her plumage, 'you're part of the team now! Isn't she, Brenda?'

'Quaaaooo,' snorted Brenda happily.

'Raaaaaaaarrrrrrk!' screeched Doris. 'You are unlike any human I have ever encountered. Now here is what our recipe says. . .'

With a trembling warble (and the best happiness she had ever known warming the insides of her belly) she read and translated the whole length of rope, from beginning to end. She pronounced each ingredient clearly and slowly, and, when Jim, Jocelyn and Brenda did not understand a particular thing, she stopped and explained what it meant.

When she had finished, Cairo Jim said in a tired but contented voice, 'Well, my friends, I think we have found our reason.'

That night, under cover of darkness, Jim, Doris and Jocelyn freed the ropes of the orange balloon, and together with Brenda the Wonder Camel and Terry's Tyroleans, they rose up towards the shimmering yellow moon, leaving the Indians of HokeyCokey with the bitter-sweet memory of the Day Their Sandra Had Returned.

16

AT THE OLD RELICS SOCIETY

In the echoing library of the Old Relics Society in Cairo, a possum-faced gentleman known as Gerald Perry Esquire blinked his marsupial-like eyes and stared at the heavy coil of rope which Jim, Doris and Brenda the Wonder Camel had thumped on the table in front of him.

'Well,' he said, rubbing his moustache this way and that. 'What's this?'

'That,' announced Jim, 'is the reason the ChaCha Muchonians danced themselves to extinction.'

'Eh? A piece of rope with feathers and bones and rags in it? You're pulling my leg.'

'No, Perry, I'm quite serious.'

Gerald Perry regarded him sceptically.

'It's a recipe,' squawked Doris.

Jim nodded. 'For Cuzco Clackersmackers.'

'Quaaoo,' snorted Brenda.

'Listen,' said Jim. 'Doris will decipher it.'

Perry sat forward and clasped his hands on the desk. 'All righty,' he said. 'I'm *dying* to hear.'

Jim uncoiled the rope and laid it along the length of the reading table, and Doris began at the beginning, waddling next to the valuable relic as she read the recipe aloud.

'Raark. Un taza miel (one cup honey)...moler jengibre (ground ginger)...treinta cucharada azúcar (thirty spoonfuls sugar)...'

'Goodness!' exclaimed Gerald Perry, his stomach churning.

'Seis moler nuez de betel (six ground betel nuts)...'

Here, Doris skipped over a clump of knots which had several colourful feathers tied in them. She continued with the next cluster.

'Poquito ambrosia (a little honeydew)...and finally, ochenta taza cacao (eighty cups chocolate).'

Gerald Perry whistled through his moustache. 'Talk about sweet,' he gasped.

'And that's for only a small ration of Clackersmackers,' said Jim.

'But I don't understand. How could a sickeningly sweet thing like this——'

'There's something else,' interrupted Cairo Jim, 'something which Sandra Panza added to her confectionery. Would you decipher it please, Doris?'

She waddled back to the clump of knots she had skipped before. Clearing her voice, she announced loudly:

'Diez cucharada arsenico.'

'Ten spoonfuls of *arsenic*,' translated Jim.

'By Hatshepsut!' said Perry. 'She...she *poisoned* them?'

'I'd say she had no idea it was poison until it was too late,' said Jim gravely.

'But why would she put it in Clackersmackers?'

'I have a theory,' the archaeologist–poet said. 'One

of Terry's Tyroleans told me that the ancient mountain-eers of Styria in south-east Austria used arsenic in miniscule doses as an energy booster. It gave them a sense of well-being, and enabled them to work longer without feeling tired. Perhaps Sandra knew of these properties, and so she put it in her Clackersmackers so her people could dance for as long as possible. I'd say she only started putting it in the recipe after they came to the top of HokeyCokey. The air up there is much thinner than in Cuzco, and she might have thought the arsenic would slow down their respiratory systems and enable them to breathe more easily. Whatever her reason, it was quite tragically disastrous.'

'Well, knock me down with a mongoose!' Perry licked his lips and stood. 'Once again, Cairo Jim, you've done extraordinarily well.'

'I had invaluable assistance,' he smiled, giving Doris and Brenda a wink.

'Would you join me for a Belzoni Whopper or two?'

'Why, thank you, Perry, but no. We'd like to get back to the Valley of the Kings as soon as possible. Doris hasn't seen it yet, and I've heard rumours that someone's digging for the tomb of Pharaoh Martenarten. *I'd* love to have a go at that.'

'Yes, yes, by all means. If you need funding again . . .'

Jim shook his patron's hand. 'Thank you, Perry, you're a champion.'

'Yes. Oh, Jim, before you go, take a look at this. I don't know what to make of it.'

He handed him a copy of the latest Society

newsletter. On the front page they read the bold heading:

DISCOVERY AT NAZCA
ARCHAEOLOGISTS BAFFLED BY STRANGE NEW LINES!

Underneath was a photograph of several archaeologists scratching their heads, obviously baffled, and then a neat drawing of the startling new phenomenon:

'Goodness,' frowned Cairo Jim. 'What on earth——?'

'It's all gibberish to me,' Doris squawked.

'Mmm,' mmmed Perry. 'It'll take 'em years to work it out.'

'Quaaooo,' snorted Brenda as Jim led her and Doris out of the library and into the warm Egyptian sunshine. The mighty Wonder Camel chuckled quietly all the way down the street as she remembered how her amigo, the last of the Inca Princes, had never been good with ploughs as a rule.

Or *had* he?

THE END

ANOTHER TALE BY GEOFFREY MCSKIMMING

CAIRO JIM AND DORIS
IN SEARCH OF MARTENARTEN
A TALE OF ARCHAEOLOGY, ADVENTURE AND ASTONISHMENT

Far away in Upper Egypt, in a place known as the Valley of the Kings, Cairo Jim (assisted by the hieroglyph-reading macaw Doris and Brenda the Wonder Camel) is searching for the lost tomb of Pharaoh Martenarten, Worshipper of the Moon and King of ancient Egypt.

It is not an easy search. Plagued by uncertainty, the dauntless trio persevere in a harsh climate made all the more worse by dust, sand and petty skulduggery.

But these are the least of their troubles. Somebody of great deviousness, treachery and manicured evil wants what they are after. And he will stop at nothing to claim it for his own!

'*A rattling good yarn.*'—MARGARET MAHY

'*Beguiling...full of implausible derring-do, historical and archaeological allusions and outrageous puns.*'
—THE AGE

'*A wonderful tale, wonderfully told...I enjoyed it immensely, especially the bits about myself.*'
—GERALD PERRY ESQUIRE

'*Comes with a Triple A rating...will have you hooked from the very first page.*'
—NSW SCHOOL MAGAZINE

'*Mr McSkimming should lay down his pen if he knows what's good for him. Arrr.*'
—CAPTAIN N. BONE

ISBN 0 340 59930 8

WOULD YOU BELIEVE EVEN ANOTHER TALE
BY GEOFFREY MCSKIMMING?

AFTER THE PUCE EMPRESS
A JOCELYN OSGOOD ADVENTURE

While on a stormbound flight to Shanghai, a mysterious old
man from Manchuria thrusts a strange object into the hand
of Jocelyn Osgood, the well-known Flight Attendant with
Valkyrian Airways. The old man inexplicably disappears in
mid-flight, leaving Jocelyn with a clue to the whereabouts
of a priceless treasure from Chinese antiquity—one that
holds the very secret to pure magic...

With advice from Cairo Jim, Jocelyn and her friend Joan
Twilight embark upon the search for the Puce Empress, a
search which takes them to China's mountainous and uncertain south.

But Gordon Slenderhead, that renowned prestidigitator,
is also after the Puce Empress, and his devious desire is
all-consuming...

*'The third in this series of exuberant comedies (is)
a fascinating over-the-top adventure...sheer
good fun...Bless you, McSkimming!'*
—AUSTRALIAN BOOKSELLER AND PUBLISHER

*'Hugely entertaining with lots of suspense, humour
and mystery...devoured at one sitting by my eleven
year old who pronounced it to be 'ace'...sure to be
a big success.'*—SOPHIE MASSON, ARMIDALE EXPRESS

'I must say Miss Osgood did very well indeed.'
—JIM OF CAIRO

*'My discarded toenail clippings have more
interesting structure to them than this latest plot of
Mr McSkimming's. Enough is surely enough! Arrr.'*
—CAPTAIN N. BONE

ISBN 0 340 58445 9

AND WHILE WE'RE AT IT,
A FURTHER TALE BY GEOFFREY MCSKIMMING

CAIRO JIM AND THE SUNKEN SARCOPHAGUS OF SEKHERET
A TALE OF MAYHEM, MYSTERY AND MOISTURE

When the manicured and devious archaeologist, Captain Neptune F. Bone, disappears in the Red Sea while diving for the lost sarcophagus of an obscure Pharaoh, that well-known archaeologist and little-known poet, Cairo Jim, is called in to try and help find him in the dark and watery depths.

Together with his companions, the noble macaw Doris and the enigmatic Brenda the Wonder Camel, he takes the plunge. They have no idea, however, that what they are about to find will become one of the most flabbergasting discoveries in the history of archaeology!

'This is McSkimming at his best, full of vile puns and impossible predicaments, and rapidly becoming an institution amongst the initiated.'
—AUSTRALIAN BOOKSELLER & PUBLISHER

'An admirable retelling of this largely unknown piece of the petticoat of History.'—GERALD PERRY ESQUIRE

'Breathtaking and unputdownable.'
—THE ZARUNDIAN ADVOCATE

'Right! That's it! You'll be hearing from my lawyers. I was never as moist as this. Arrr.'—CAPTAIN N. BONE

ISBN 0 340 62222 9

SURPRISE, SURPRISE! ANOTHER TALE
BY GEOFFREY MCSKIMMING

XYLOPHONES ABOVE ZARUNDI
A CHAOTIC TALE OF MELODY

While on a stopover in the mysterious African country of
Zarundi, Jocelyn Osgood—that well-known Valkyrian
Airways Flight Attendant and "good friend" of Cairo Jim—
becomes unwittingly embroiled in the theft of a priceless
royal tiara. She and her companions find themselves thrown
into a world of subtle chaos which carries them across an
intriguing and colourful landscape as they try desperately
to locate the stolen regalia and two renegade Tropical
Xylophonists...

*'If Mr McSkimming's tongue were more firmly in his
cheek he'd risk permanent speech impediment.'*
—AUSTRALIAN BOOK REVIEW

*'Gosh, I knew she was dauntless, but this takes the
shergold cake.'*—JIM OF CAIRO

*'The irrepressible McSkimming is at it again...
followers of the Cairo Jim comedy/mystery series will
cheer this latest outrageous cocktail of adventure, puns
and scrambled history.'*—MARGARET DUNKLE

'I couldn't pick it up. Arrr.'—CAPTAIN N. BONE

ISBN 0 340 62245 8

CAIRO JIM AND THE ALABASTRON OF FORGOTTEN GODS
A TALE OF DISPOSABLE DESPICABLENESS

A seemingly ordinary vase is stolen from the Greek Archaeological Museum by a figure swathed in mystery. But the vase—an ancient alabastron—holds a secret: a potent force within it that must NOT be allowed to escape!

It is up to Cairo Jim (that well-known archaeologist and little-known poet) and friends to track down the thief, before the alabastron's mysterious contents are unleashed upon the modern world...

'Quite possibly the most amazing tale yet...my heart was racing from the adventure and my sides were aching from so much laughter.'
—JOCELYN OSGOOD V.O.S.

'An over-the-top action-packed adventure filled with crime, mystery, intrigue...outrageous puns, it is rollicking good fun.'—VIEWPOINT

'A brilliant thriller...will whet the reader's appetite for more.'—SOUTHSIDE CHRONICLE, ACT

'Mr McSkimming would be better to sneeze into a handkerchief and have that *published. I thought it wretched and banal. Arrr.'*—CAPTAIN N. BONE

ISBN 0 340 62187 7

CAIRO JIM'S BUMPER BOOK OF FLABBERGASTING FRAGMENTS

INCLUDING POEMS INSPIRED BY THE LEGENDARY JOCELYN HIEROGLYPHS

Now at last, in response to countless requests from the rich and famous, the discerning and the desperate, is a collection of poetry by that well-known archaeologist and little-known poet, Cairo Jim. Together with some recently discovered stories from the world of Jim, Doris and Brenda (including a rare Melodious Tex story), and a foreword by Gerald Perry Esquire (not to mention riddles, puzzles, tongue tanglers and Mrs Amun-Ra's Recipes of Delectability), this collection is a worthy addition to the personal library of any true aficionado of the Cairo Jim 'mysteries of history'.

HOURS OF FUN AND DISTRACTION!

'How I wish I'd had a copy of this to while away the timeliness when we were travelling to Samothraki. A wonderful and witty tome.'—EURIPIDES DOODAH

'Packed with puns, photos, poetry and puzzles ...hours of fun.'—VIEWPOINT

'Bringing history to life in a startling manner... McSkimming's style is inspirational to young readers.'
—SOUTHSIDE CHRONICLE, ACT

'The perfect book to read on a long journey...more entertaining than the xylophone.'—ELSPETH KAMITONGO

'I would rather watch grass growing than read this horrendous collection of drivel. Arrr.'
—CAPTAIN N. BONE

ISBN 0 7336 0383 1

WELL, WELL, WELL: A FURTHER TALE
BY GEOFFREY MCSKIMMING

CAIRO JIM AND THE QUEST FOR THE QUETZAL QUEEN
A MAYAN TALE OF MARVELS

Strange paintings have come to light in ancient Mexican pyramids and temples. Is the mysterious painted woman the actual Quetzal Queen? Did she really reign for almost 800 years? What has the sudden disappearance of Fifi Glusac (the famous contortionist and harmonica player) got to do with it?

Cairo Jim, that well-known archaeologist and little-known poet, with his friends Doris the macaw and Brenda the Wonder Camel, finds himself faced with *another* flabbergasting mystery from times past...

'Extraordinary... a wonderful mix of playful phrases and tricky witticisms... a classic adventure story of kidnappings and trapdoors and the ultimate quest.'
—AUSTRALIAN BOOKSELLER AND PUBLISHER

'A stunning account of a little-known story.'
—DELVING (THE JOURNAL OF THE INTERNATIONAL MAYAN ARCHAEOLOGICAL WAYFARERS ANTIQUARIAN GROUP)

'A gem of a Jim! A great addition to the Cairo Jim chronicles.'—MILLICENT SPULE, MA (HONS) HITT LETT OPE

'I wish I'd been there with him, all right.'
—JOCELYN OSGOOD VOS

'I would prefer to have my eyebrows plucked by an orang-utan devoid of tweezers. This is truly dire! Arrr.'
—CAPTAIN N. BONE

ISBN 0 7336 0293 2

AN ICY TALE BY GEOFFREY MCSKIMMING

ASCENT INTO ASGARD
A JOCELYN OSGOOD JAUNT

While stopping over in Norway, Joan Twilight buys a rusty old hammer for her friend, Jocelyn Osgood (the well-known Flight Attendant with Valkyrian Airways and "good friend" of Cairo Jim), whom she knows has a minor lust for antiquities.

With advice from Cairo Jim, Jocelyn and Joan seek out Professor Kurt Snerdforst, an expert on things now forgotten. Jocelyn decides to return the hammer to an isolated location in Norway's cold, northern regions.

Slowly, however, the shadows of an ancient world begin to creep across their journey, as the hammer proves to be much more than a worthless, dusty relic...

> 'If you like bizarre adventures, flamboyant characters, great plots and hilarious encounters... then the Jocelyn Osgood/Cairo Jim adventures are for you.'—AUSTRALIAN BOOKSELLER AND PUBLISHER

> 'Another dauntless episode from this remarkable woman's life, written with breathless whimsy and aplomb.'—THE INTREPID WOMAN'S QUARTERLY

> 'An unlikely, amazing and hysterically funny Norwegian adventure... short, sharp chapters, snappy dialogue and endless fast-paced action... great fun.'—READING TIME

> 'Wonderful ... not unlike a good champagne—it's the froth and bubbles that make it special.'—MAGPIES

> 'The only good thing about this bit of literature is that many trees were destroyed to create it. Rainforests are sinister and Mr McSkimming is even more so. Arrr.'
> —CAPTAIN N. BONE

ISBN 0 7336 0294 0

CAIRO JIM AND THE SECRET
SEPULCHRE OF THE SPHINX
A TALE OF INCALCULABLE INVERSION

When that well-known archaeologist and little-known poet, Cairo Jim, and his friends Doris the macaw, Brenda the Wonder Camel, and Jocelyn Osgood make the 'find of the century', a new enemy on the scene sets out to discredit Jim and destroy his hard-won reputation...

Another mind-blowing mystery of history from the master of archaeological humour and suspense, Geoffrey McSkimming.

THE BIGGEST DISCOVERY OF ALL THE
CAIRO JIM MYSTERIES OF HISTORY!

'Yet another outrageous adventure, this is classic McSkimming, complete with a devious plot that will keep pages turning until the very end. Readers with a taste for parody are finding his exploits addictive. This one is top class.'
—AUSTRALIAN BOOKSELLER AND PUBLISHER

'There is no hope for the world if Mr McSkimming is allowed to continually produce such slanderous bilge as this. Arrr.'—CAPTAIN N. BONE

ISBN 0 7336 0579 6

Coming soon:

Cairo Jim and the Chaos from Knossos
Cairo Jim and the Rorting of Rameses' Relic
Jocelyn Osgood in Bollywood